THE GIANT'S CAUSEWAY

CONSTANTINE O'DONNELL

ISBN: 978-1-63950-230-1 (sc)
ISBN: 978-1-63950-231-8 (e)

Writers Apex

Gateway Towards Success

8063 MADISON AVE #1252
Indianapolis, IN 46227
+13176596889
www.writersapex.com

SERIES 1

This book has been tampered with by the Real I.R.A. I went on the internet and they infiltrated it. They wiped some of my work…it does not matter. The aliens are killing the perpetrators with Leukaemia… the Real Irish Army are my brothers and sisters…they will protect my family of Andrea and kids.

This book is dedicated to the Canadian, Andrea Garbula. She is the most attractive woman I have ever had the pleasure of not hitting on when I had the chance lol I want her to be my wife. I asked her would she marry me if I was rich and she said maybe…that was all the inspiration I needed to persevere and become as rich as I could. I am now a Billionaire. I hope she will marry me.

This book is going to be an absolute clinker!

I am going to tell you all about my life as an alien.

We are from Pachsion. We do not adhere to human laws. We are above them. We are going to be inexplicably direct in our ruling of earth. We are going to be the true lifeforce on the planet. We are not going to be a quasi-essential law bringing nation. We are the rulers of the universe. Con is our King! Bipolar has been used to discredit him. The psychoanalysis is about to end. We are dead against psychotropic medication. Schizophrenia does not exist. Schizophrenia is the spirit world talking to the living. We are not going to stand by and watch the psychiatrists kill all the humans with the ability to talk to the dead.

There are millions of humans with this gift. There will not be any mental asylums on planet earth by the time we are finished. They will all be closed!

We have been around the countries of earth for millions of years. We have watched you grow. Aliens put life on planet earth. We are your brethren, there are no other aliens in the universe who have the advanced technology to do what we do. We have spaceships and can be at earth in seconds from our home world. We live 100 billion light years away!

There is going to be a new world order. We will rewrite the laws on earth. There will be the death penalty for killing and raping another human being! That will be the only laws on earth. There will be no need for anymore laws. There will be no need for judges or lawyers. The police on earth will no longer be bullying civilians. They are going to be extinct. No police on earth. The military will demilitarize in all countries. No more soldiering or killing in the name of war. Prince Harry tried to glamourize it, killing 25 people on his computer screen, it is like a computer game to him. Not thinking of the pain and suffering he is causing when he hits innocent people. This is not going to be tolerated. There are going to be good people in charge of each and every country. There will be no more royalty anywhere on earth. The Commonwealth of Britain is over!!! I am from an oppressed nation. We have great sense of identity! The Brits tried to kill us all in a mass genocide which they called the great famine. It was orchestrated by the British government. The I.R.A have been fighting the British Army for a century. They have won!!! It is a great honour for me to announce to the world that I did my bit for them! I took over Shannon Airport without a gun. I pretended to have Bipolar to get away from the clutches of the law. It worked!!! George W. Bush was landing. I penetrated security stoned as hell! I was also tripping on acid. I am going to make a movie out of this escapade. It will be shot in a couple of hours. It will be narrated what I was thinking. I am going to be the greatest ruler the universe has ever seen. I am going to Pachsion after I finish ruling earth. My family that I leave behind will rule the earth forever!

There a few things that really irk me. One is homosexuality. There is no such thing among men. Women have an emotional side that allows them to feel this bond with another women. It is just disgusting among men. As aliens we have watched it evolve. Men become infatuated with other men when they are in close proximity for long periods of time. They idolize them. That is not homosexuality. Anal sex is made up to make it feel normal. That is where your shit comes out! Women are designed to have a cock inside them. Men are not you cock sucking homos lol.

The next thing that really pisses me off is a little thing known as racism. It's an English thing. They think they are superior to the rest of the human race. It spread through the centuries to different parts of Commonwealth. They are the most vile people in the universe. We have watched them and their royal bullshit for centuries. We have put an I.R.A man in charge of the planet. We love how that will go down with their fucking arrogant attitude.

The Pleiades are not containing any aliens like the bullshit spread on the internet. Con even believed it and thought that is where we came from. We have been talking to Con since he was born. We have been putting suggestions and thoughts in his head from birth. Con is the smartest individual in the universe. We have waited 3 million years for him to arrive. Con still cannot believe it himself. We are the most advanced aliens in the universe. The universe has thousands of planets with alien lifeforms on them. They are all human. Earth is the youngest planet in the universe. That is why we are here. They have reached their final stage of evolution. They cannot advance any further without our help. Tesla was so advanced for his time. We had a hand in this. Elon Musk will be the second richest man on the planet after Con. They will be allies. There will be no competing. Jeff Bezos will also be one of the richest men on the planet. He will also be an ally of ours. The space exploration will stop. The alien race has come to them. They no longer have to search for them. We heard Con's poetry on the other side of the universe. He put it on the internet and didn't receive a penny. He thought people should read it. He is the biggest Genius in the universe. We are so resolute in our quest to find a suitable partner for Con. His dream of having 3 or 4 women as partners is absolutely ridiculous. He is hearing our opinion now for the first time as he reads this. What do you think Con? Do you think one good woman is enough to satisfy your urges? We know that he has an insatiable appetite for women. It's an alien thing! LOL.

Anywho, as my cousin Niall aka Styley would say. There are bigger things afoot. We must get all the worlds governments to agree to our new system for the earth. That will take some doing. They will all demand proof of our existence. It has already happened Con when he did an interview for a local Donegal newspaper. They're a bit behind the times here. They need to get out and explore the world a bit more. They wouldn't print the interview because he couldn't prove to them of our existence. Idiots!!! They'll be in the movie as retards!

After all is said and done, we will start to assess the world for compatibility to our technology. We will introduce free living costs e.g electricity. We know this is boring the life out of Con writing this. He is a fucking high octane guy. Just read his book iCon wildman101. Back to the wine Con!!

I am not one bit perturbed by the incessant betrayal of people like Prince Harry. They live an opulent life and believe the world owes them something. He was such a fucking idiot throughout his life. No wonder he was the Spare!

The I.R.A are not that far through the looking glass as not to see they have been vilified in the world media for years because of the Brits. They will now be seen as Freedom fighters! Their songs and stories will be heard on the world stage. There will be no more talk of terrorism. They were fighting for their country to have a new beginning. The unusual activity in Derry will not happen anymore. There will be an unfounded beginning of unusual funding from me when I'm a Trillionaire. This won't be a one off thing. I am going to build Derry up into a world tourism destination. The people deserve it. My Grandmother owned a bar on Magazine Street. My Grandfather from Derry played for Cork city and the Republic of Ireland in football. I'm so proud of them both. I don't have a great relationship with all my cousins on that side of the family but I want to. This book will hopefully help with that.

I will never be in a mental asylum again! They are the most vile people in the universe if you fall out with them. At the beginning, they loved me. All the female nurses would flirt with me. All the male nurses would adopt me as the hard man. This went on for years until the I.R.A put an end to it. They took it upon themselves to ridicule me and decided they needed to put me in my place. I was too powerful for them. They can get fucked. If anything happens me.

I will not be on my own for very much longer. I will have women in my life. They will be really, really, really gorgeous and funny! I will not be alarmed when its bedtime. They all can take me to bed. We will have so much fun! There will be lots of sex. Forever!!! If you are reading this and would like to sleep with me, get yourself to Sint Maarten & The South of France. I will be open to all beautiful women. If you have a brain, then I might have a child with you. I will give you a million dollars to have and to look after my child. I will not be in the family loop but I will keep contact. I want lots of children. The aliens are telling me to do this. I am building an empire. The O'Donnell reign will happen again. I am going to buy Sint Maarten and call it 'Constantine'. The airport will be renamed 'O'Donnell airport'. There will be a bronze statue of me with my Samurai swords and a foot-long erection. I will be naked in the statue with muscles galore. It will be the most photographed statue in the world in a few years time. Women everywhere will be swinging off my erection. It will be a welcome to Sint Maarten!

There won't be any more crime on planet earth. It will all cease. There will be lots of money for everyone. I cannot wait to divide the worlds wealth up between everybody! It will not be long before this happens. I am joining all the wealthy people of this world together. They will decide on everything that happens with their money. I will be the ringleader of a very powerful elite. There will be no bitching or moaning about rich people. They looked out for me all in the South of France. They are good people. They are very smart! You can learn from them.

We will always be part of earth after this takeover. Con will not be here for long. He will die in 40 years time. That will be a joyous occasion. He is coming home with his mission complete. He is our King. We cannot wait until he meets his wife Gotta. She is the most beautiful on our planet. She loves other women too. She is in a relationship with another women for the next 40 years until Con gets here. This is news to him as well. We are revealing everything to him for the first time as he writes this book. We did not want to bore him. He is SO intelligent.

Con's sister Margaret is very, very, very stubborn. She did not treat him well growing up. She was always jealous. She calls him Big Con mocking him. He arrived home from Mallorca with nowhere to live. He pitched a tent with his brother and his brother's girlfriends help. They bought him some food. He had no money either. Catherine bought him cigarettes to help him relax. She is a beautiful woman. My brother really done well for himself. I'm proud of my brother. The only thing is, he is terrible at keeping contact. It fucks me off so much!

There will not be any problems with the I.R.A for the British people. They will all be under my control. They will be my security all over the world. They will be armed. The only armed people on the planet. They will not be on CONSTANTINE. There will be BRITISH special forces armed as well on Constantine. I have an affinity with them. My cousin James McGilloway aka Moggy, wanted me to join the British army with him. I seriously considered it. I was 17 and not doing well at school. I said no and he laughed. He said to me "Too I.R.A?" He was laughing his head off. He joined and ended up in the Parachute regiment. I was really proud of him.

I am going to be the most constitutional inept person in the universe when I get my US greencard. I want to be an American citizen and come and go as I please. I will be a Hollywood action hero. I dreamed as a kid to be a stuntman. Burt Reynolds was a hero of mine growing up.

As I have said, there will be no crime but there will also be no love anymore. It does not exist. There's infatuation with each other at the beginning of every relationship. People mistake this for love. It wears thin after a while. Human species is not designed to live with one person for their whole life. We did not design you like this. It will end. People will have multiple partners and the children will stay with their mothers. Other men will bring up other men's children. It will be interesting for the children to have such a varied upbringing. The mothers will be attentive and womanly for their men.

There is going to be other species from other Galaxies coming to earth to control the people. They will be good rulers. Do not worry. We are the most peaceful species in the universe and the new people that are coming will be so enthralled by their surroundings that they will inspire you to be happy to be from such a brilliant planet. There is not going to be any war anymore.

If there is any grievances with this new world order, you must be an asshole!!! We are your God. We designed you. We have watched for thousands of years as you evolved. The people living with the Dinosaurs were the bravest ever to roam the planet. Imagine living in that era lol.

There is going to be a magnificent eclipse of the moon and everyone on earth will rejoice. This will be monumental. All space exploration is no longer necessary. NASA is finished. It is not needed anymore. The American people will no longer be concerned about whether there is something in the universe that can kill them. The internet is full of scare mongering. We read it. We can read everything that is put up on the internet every second of the day. That is how advanced we are!

There will be no Kangaroos in Australia anymore. They will all be exterminated. They are a pests. Snakes all over the world will be exterminated as well. We will show you how to do this. Rats as well. They are filthy things. Con has been told by his fucking asshole of a dope smoking neighbour that Rathmullan is infested by rats. He is paranoid. Lay off the weed Martin.

Assholes who litter will be killed lol just kidding. Do not litter! Earth will be a paradise. Be proud of it!

There is going to be a different type of TV program. There will not be any crap on television worldwide. It will be intelligent programming. Hollywood will no longer exaggerate life. All movies will be based on stories from the most wildest humans. There are millions of them. Earth has the biggest concentration of crazy people in the universe. Con should know, he's the craziest. We designed him that way. We have been telling him to do mad things all his life. He is an adrenaline junkie.

There is going to be a wild side to all his children. They will be great craic. They will be the smartest kids in school. And their mothers will be the most beautiful, elegant models on the planet. Con is going to begin jogging this April 2024 and he will lose all the fucking weight he put on in the mental asylum. It has been annoying him for the couple of years. He doesn't eat a whole lot AND he doesn't drink beer anymore. That will change when he gets to the Caribbean. He will enjoy a few beers for breakfast watching the news on TV lol he's getting older now. His women will enjoy cocktails with him. They will have house staff and not be worried about such trivialities as house cleaning. His house staff will be very well treated.

There will not be any disobedience from any human in the near future. All hoodlums will be severely reprimanded. There will be a prison in Australia. It will be the biggest in the universe. It will be in the centre of the continent. Right where it is hottest. There will be no air conditioning in the prison. Prison guards will not be used. Everything will be computerised. That is all we are saying.

All prisons at present are going to be emptied when we take over. Everyone will be given a second chance. The prison in Australia will be able to hold everybody in the planet should this necessity arise. We are only joking!! We know that the crime is all because of poverty. Once poverty is cancelled there will be no reason to commit a crime. There will be no jealous people.

If there is a reason to be imprisoned. Then…kill yourself. It will be a lot better than going to our prison. There will not be any reprieve. You will go there for life. That includes any terrorism and especially thievery. We detest it. Con is a bit of a thief. He used to sell the paint from the Merchant Navy boats lol it was fun. He used the money for beer. It's an old Merchant Navy tradition.

There is going to be a lack of people doing menial jobs. These jobs will be highly paid. There are going to be no sugary sweets on the planet anymore. People will only brush their teeth every couple of days or if they are going somewhere special. There is a ridiculous amount of money spent on cosmetics on earth. Women will no longer wear make-up. It ruins it for men when they see you in the morning. Con nearly puked when he looked at his fuckbuddy in the morning. She had a totally different look to her. She went crazy when he inadvertently said "Ugh!" She fucking hit the roof. It was because of all her drinking. She was all blotchy with red marks all over her face. Con got out of there. She was fucking mental. We reached a plateau with Con when he was with her. The sex was fantastic but the lights were out lol ah no she wasn't that bad looking. Con wouldn't be with her if she was. He has never been with an out of this world dirt bag. They hold no charm for him. He is a ladies man, there's no question about that. Con has had so many women that he doesn't know how many he has slept with. We think it's hilarious!

There is going to be a law around all alcohol. It will say "Get it into you!!" LOL. Con loves to drink. It's his release. The drugs are more recreational for him when he is in company.

I think there will be a large induction of Seafarers into Maritime colleges all over the world. This is very good. The world is so exciting when seen this way. You look forward to visiting new places and meeting new women.

I know of many women who would love to have my baby BUT I am very wary of who brings up my kids. My kids will be unruly and a little wild. My mother was a vixen but mostly could control me. She was a pretty cool mother.

My father was my idol growing up. He let me down SO much when he sided with psychiatrists. He enjoyed being my superior again and would not relinquish control. He inspired lots of my poetry "Resentment of control, and fear of its loss, is a meal you feel made tastier, with an inadequate bitter sauce!" That was about him.

My poetry is one of a kind. It is SO intelligent. It is inspired by earth but talked to me from Pachsion. They would like school kids to learn them. It will open the world to them. They will want to travel and write themselves.

I have only bits of memories in my heart. There will not be a distant memory unturned when I am once again in the Caribbean. I fell in love with the place when I was yachting. It is so cool there. I was poor and the locals gave me free drugs.

God, Shrove is only a little place BUT there are so many intelligent people there. The Hegarty's from the bottom of Shrove are the brainiest I have met in the world.

My sea going career is over. I'm not bothered. I achieved Captain status which was my goal. It was only for a week on a Superyacht called Anedigmi. The Captain, ex-policeman.

John McConelogue is not as smart as he thinks. He is a bit arrogant.

My Drunken Duck years are going to be remembered in my future autobiographies. I have very little memory of it BUT the aliens are going to remind me. I look forward to it.

There will not be any women on my yacht, good luck to that idea. I could not imagine being on a yacht without women. I would not have done the job if there was only men. They made my life SO wonderful. They were from all over the world. I have such good time for hungry women lol just kidding. I like mine thin. It is fucking disgusting shagging a fat woman. I've done it a couple of times AND afterwards thought a wank would have been more enjoyable. Fuck sake. How do women expect to turn their men on with flab fucking hanging everywhere? Listen up women. Get thin!

Us aliens do not care about hurting feelings. The earth is too soft. All this mental health bullshit is over. Every asshole crying about the state of his mental health. It fucking pisses Con off SO much!!!

There is going to be a lovely lagoon somewhere in this world that I can swim naked with my women. My yacht crew will look out for them. They will be the most professional yacht crew on this planet. I will pay them handsomely. They will have time for time. I will not be caring about the change over of crew. It is abusive at the minute. It is going to change. I will make sure of it.

I am going to bring about world peace. The Dalai Lama will shut his cunting mouth. He is NOT a spiritual leader. It is bullshit!

There will be no more religion. Con thought of this himself because of his travels. We did not inspire him. He is SO adept in his analysis of the entire planet and he has only seen a fraction of it. That will change and people like Prince Harry will no longer take up the limelight for stupid things like the Invictus games. I'm only joking. I was impressed by that. It inspired me to be an alien lol.

There is going to be a prolific amount of authors in this world by the time I am finished. They will all be using my publisher. They will become the biggest self-publishing outfit on the planet. They will expand. They have been so nice to me.

All movies made about me will win Oscars. I love the movies. They have inspired my life.

There is going to be a new world order for everything. Right down to wiping your ass lol just kidding! That will always be the same. Not like the ridiculous conversation I heard on the Joe Rogan podcast one night, discussing a better way to clean your ass!! Fuck sake.

There are so many comedians on this planet. Joe Rogan is not one of them. Only joking, I enjoy him! I love his podcast. It gets me to sleep at night. I'm not the only one. I heard other people, young in particular, say that they listen at night when they go to bed.

There is going to be a new world order in sports. All sport will be amateur. There be no multi million pound soccer stars. Kids will aspire to be professional people. Like Engineers and gaslighters lol that's what they are doing to me at present in Rathmullan. They think I am trying to take over their little buttfuck of a town. I couldn't be bothered! It wouldn't be hard.

Fiona Mellon inspired me to take on the Big Pharmaceutical companies. I will take them down. It has been my biggest fight. The aliens, who are also my brothers and sisters, have told me that I have succeeded in alerting lots of mental patients of the dangerous poison the psychiatrists are peddling. The Doctors are fucking scumbags. I heard one woman plead with a Doctor to take her in to the mental asylum because she was suicidal. The Doctor upped her medication and told her she would be fine. She was a Bumbleweed from Moville. I told Scissorhands this on another fucking admission when we were both in. She thanked me for my concern BUT could not give a shit!! It's common in their family! Fucking Loserville!!

The woman committed suicide a couple of weeks later. That Doctor should be struck off. Suicide will be common when we are in control. There will be counselling for the weak people AND there will be not one bit of medication. Suicide will be stamped out in a few years time. This will happen when we get rid of all the deadwood.

There is not going to be a public domain like Twitter or Facebook for very much longer. Just kidding! I enjoy them. I will buy Facebook and you will be able to write whatever the hell you want on it. There will be no law on it. It will be so easy to run! I will enjoy owning it. Twitter will be the same. I will speak with Elon. Change of plan…6 months later…only writing it now. I am opening my own Social media group.

Football, is my favourite sport. I love playing it. I am getting too old now to play. My knees would not take the pounding and rigorous twisting. I'll settle for light jogging.

I am not going to be an astronaut anymore. It is SO scary looking to me now. I was fearless growing up. At sea, I took SO many chances. I nearly drowned a ton of times. From falling overboard to swimming drunk. It was lots of fun BUT one little cramp and you are at the bottom of the ocean. Fucking mental cases that done it with me are just as bad lol.

There is now going to be multimillion euro playgrounds all over this planet. They will have bars and restaurants. The kids will be minded while the parents indulge. Drink driving will be allowed and smoking marijuana as well. People will be told keep their speed to 30 kilometres per hour when you're smoking and drinking. Anybody caught speeding by my security will be shipped off to Australia without reprieve. That's how serious we feel about it. We are making the world a lot more liveable in. Con has been arrested SO many times he doesn't remember them all. The Gardai Siochana are so corrupt, they made up a load of charges so he would go to jail. The Judge wouldn't believe them. It was funny as fuck!!!

I am going to be getting up every morning when I hit Sint Maarten and roll a big fat spliff. It is going to be so wonderful. I will take Cocaine in the afternoon and go for a drive in my little 4x4.

There is never going to be another distance like the one we are travelling to visit earth. It will take us seconds in our spaceships. The earth will never stop loving us. We know the future!

Down and out is what people are saying to Con in the local shop, lidl. They are fucking are waster cunts. Little fucking Derrymen making snide comments about writing a book and sitting with your feet up! They have no idea how hard he worked!

Lidl is my go to for groceries. I have devised a simple diet were I don't put on any calories. It is going to be the diet of everybody that lives on their own. It is so simple. Just kidding. Eat what you want! But take care of your weight people.

I will not be subjected to my mothers suicidal reign over me. She fucking called the Guards on me a couple of times and will NOT believe me that I am over all this mental illness bullshit. She will not read the true story!

My father caused me to nearly commit suicide a heap of times.

In Derry, lots of little idiots are giving me shit. They repeat things from the hardmen in the RA. They are not going to beat me. The one that annoys me the most is "All eyes!" They look at me in the carpark returning home from a long voyage and walk into me as I'm going home, with my bag on my back and give me the mean eye. When I look back at them with a fucking pissed off look. They stare at me and say "All eyes!" In other words, I have nothing to back it up. I could have broke the fucker's neck. It pissed me off after all the fucking people in Palma were welcoming me as an I.R.A man. They were shouting in my hostel door…"Up the RA!!!" It happened about 7 or 8 times. I didn't know what the fuck was going on.

No way am I putting up with this shit!!!

There will only be movies about real life. No more space odyssey or sci fi. There will be lots of horror stories but they will be based on real events.

Like I love everything about earth, the aliens do too. They hear, feel, see and understand everything like me. I am their King.

My brother and sister will not be discouraged from the limelight when I am on the world stage. My brother will be a famous musician. His lyrics are out of this world intelligent. His new wife is super smart as well.

The aliens will be so dedicated to earth. They are so proud that I have succeeded in my mission. If things had not worked out for me, I would still be returning to Pachsion but earth would never have known and you all would become extinct. We would have let the planet run its course. You are an experiment. The real people are on our planet. You are from Pachsion bred in a test tube. Your star sign is Pyrex! That's one of Con's jokes. He was inspired by test tube and it came rushing back to him.

Now, people of earth, you must realise how lucky you are to have Con O'Donnell on the planet! He has been all over Islands in the Caribbean and has lots of stories to tell. We will remind him of them.

There is going to be lots of Superyachts built. The cost will decrease. All the movie stars and rich millionaires will be buying them. It's a great way to live. Con enjoyed it immensely. Nearly as much as cuming on Fiona Mellon's face lol that's who Flo was in the book.

Niall Mellon is being vilified in the press in Ireland for drunk and disorderly's. I know how he feels. They cut me to shreds too in an article about me spitting on the floor in front of this dickhead who was insulting me in the hospital A&E in Letterkenny General hospital. I was making shapes to fight him. I was only messing. I saw the travellers at it on TV. Spitting on the ground and looking at them with a mean look as if to say "C'mon, I'm not afraid of you!" I thought it was funny. There was a load of people there. Another time in the A&E in Letterkenny. A guy fucking insulted me, gaslighting me. Saying abusive shit and not looking at me. I wasn't in the mood. I stared the cunt out. He was 3 or 4 seats away with his girlfriend. She grabbed his hand and said warning him "Let's get out of here before it becomes Beirut!" I never broke my stare! They ran like fuck! See Derrymen, I am all eyes! Lol but them 2 little cunts know I can back it up even at my age. You better watch your fuckin step around me!

There is an inordinate amount of Cocaine in Columbia. It will be all over the world by the time we are finished. Columbia will feed the world with Cocaine.

If you are in any way a prude, do not read this book! I do not want to hear fucking imbeciles telling me they were insulted by this little bit or that little bit. We are from a different world. We are here to take over the planet. We know there will be humans who will not like what we are saying. They can get fucked lol. We are so fucking happy that Con became a writer. It wasn't in the stars. Oh yes it was. We designed him that way. He has a photographic memory. He remembers everything like it just happened. Even when drunk!

Conor McElhinney is a chav lol just kidding. His name is Mac Sea in iCon wildman101. He will want to sue me when he reads this but he won't. He'll enjoy the fame. We go back a long way!

Shane McElhinney is also a chav lol just kidding. His name is Mac Eas in iCon. He will also want to sue me when he reads this but he won't. He'll enjoy the fame too. He has such a fucking temper on him lol.

There is going to be loving for every human on the planet. We will help humans explore their sexuality. Religion on earth stifled the life out of sex. It was crazy watching how it all evolved. Con just asked a very pertinent question. Why didn't we step in sooner? We always believed that earth needed to evolve like it has. No one ruler. Lots of nations. It was so cool to watch. We have a live feed to our planet. All our children tune into it. They love Hollywood. The elders not so much. They are like Con. They detest people who exaggerate. You will never hear anybody exaggerate around Con. He will bring them up on it!

I've just had the mental health services call. They are locking me up again. They are trying to get me on medication. I told them about 3 children at the local lidl Supermarket saying to me as I was walking in the door of the shop "Shout Tiocfaidh ar la!!!" They don't believe me. This is going to the mattresses lol as the Italian Mafia say!

I am so annoyed by the mental health services. They are so corrupt. This is going to be fun!! I can't wait to pit my intelligence against the cunts. 3 weeks of torturing them. Then a tribunal. Lying cunts..they are as bad the British with their oppression.

1 week done. That is all they kept me in for. They are proper assholes!!! It's another chapter of my life. One that needs ignoring. I met a few nice women in there. We had good fun! There was even a suggestion of a threesome by Miss Dandy!

I am out of this world delighted to be a free man once more. I bought 5 bottles of red wine to celebrate.

They are nearly all gone now lol!!

Back to the real talk.

I am an alien. I will always be an alien. I will be in the history books of every country. There is not a world like earth in the universe. It is so combustible. Earthquakes, Hurricanes, mud slides everything!!! We do know the future of earth and it is fabulous. Earth will party like there is no tomorrow. Every country on earth will have a brilliant future. People will travel everywhere.

There will be an overture of life involved in every aspect of human existence. It will be an extroverted convenience lol.

There are humans with unlimited intelligence in this world BUT they are side lined because of it. This will no longer be the case. They will be celebrated!!

There is going to be no vitriol of ambience in the new world. There will be wine and dance!!

I'm happy to be writing the new world order. It is exciting!!

There is going to be a very lucrative people in the Irish sector. They will come from far and wide. There will be no racism like what Con experienced as a young sailor.

Our world is magnanimous in defeat lol no we're not. We reign supreme!

We live forever. People on earth can not imagine how we live. They will be intrigued forever about our world. Con is coming home after this mission. It has been the wildest ride of our historical journey in this universe. We cannot be intrigued by anything that he does lol we are just kidding. He is the wildest of our planet. Everybody adores him. Kids want to be him!! Women want to sleep with him and men want him as a drinking buddy!!

There will be no paraplegic or handicap children any more. They will be terminated in the womb. It is not fair on them to live a life of limited existence. It is one of Con's pet peve's. Why children should be brought into this world when they have a death sentence on them already.

I am going to be the mightiest ruler ever. Oh yes, I will!!

This is the beginning of my career as an author. I will have lots of books. The alien race whom I'm part of will inundate the world at large with my witticisms and anecdotal accounts of my life on this planet. There is going to be an unusual amount of authors coming through from Ireland. All the mental patients are writing down their experiences at the hands of patronising nurses and Doctors in the mental asylums.

We on Pachsion have been waiting for millions of years for this to happen. It is in our folklore. There have been millions of books written on Con's account of his life. He has nearly ended it so many times. We knew that he would survive to tell the tale BUT he did not know this. It has been the wildest ride known to man. He has his own doubts. Even he thinks there are wilder humans than him BUT we can let him know there aren't. He is the wildest!!!

There will be an inexplicable deviant among the people WHO will not like him! These people are jealous of him. Even his own cousin Styley is very jealous of him. He went into the life of a sailor at a very young age. He used to travel with his father up the Foyle into Derry when he was only 6 years of age. His memories of them days are burned into his mind. He used to play with the radars and go and visit the engine room. The engineers job never appealed to him. He enjoyed engineering at school immensely BUT he wanted to be in charge lol don't we all!!!

I am at one with him. We are an unusual type of alien. We enjoy alcohol and narcotics just as much as the wildest humans. Alcohol and drugs will be common place on our new version of earth. It is going to be the greatest place in the universe to live, hands down!

We are writing a very unusual book. It is short little paragraphs with lots of information contained in each of them.

There is going to be an inordinate amount of Gardai Siochana handing in their notice. We as aliens cannot wait to see this happen. They have been very ignorant to Con in the last few years. They tried to put him in prison. He is too fucking smart for them lol so are we!

If there is any Gardai who would like a signed autograph from Con then we advise you to kiss his big behind lol just kidding. We are going to bring a new world order.

We have just about enough intelligence to bring about world peace lol just kidding. This was always going to happen.

Con still can't believe it is really happening. He is the coolest fucking man in the universe. He has always been. Every woman he meets wants to sleep with him. Young and old. They all fantasise about him. During his last and final admission to the Letterkenny unit aka mental asylum, the women were all around him. One of them even suggested a threesome. Right up his street lol he's had a couple of them. He had one threesome with two hookers in Nice, SoF(South of France). It was very mechanical. Pulling off condoms and putting on fresh ones after sticking his cock into each hooker. Not much fun! He prefers all the juices flowing inexplicably, incestuously lol just kidding! Incest is not best lol old Leprechaun Leper aka Lepy will agree with him on that point. He shagged his younger sister when he was 14 years of age. Dirty cunt!

All the Bumbleweeds that Con talks about in iCon wildman101 are not one bit brave enough to have a fight with Con. Con is trained in several martial arts. He is fucking deadly!!! Remember that when you go to give him abuse.

I have been through the worst 20 years you could not even imagine. I thought I would never get out of that fucking mental asylum in

Letterkenny. It is a little piece of hell. If only people would realise it without Con having to go back in there and tell them. He went along with our plan to be locked up again. It was very well thought out by you Pachsion! Of course, it was Con!

There is going to be a lot of O'Donnells in this world stepping up to the podium and announcing that they are proud to have the same name as Red Hugh and Con O'Donnell!

I am victim to several types of abuse here in Rathmullan. The local shop is where I get my morning coffee and they are victimising me. Proper stuck up bitches!!!

If I have been to all the countries on this planet, then I would have been out on a limb! Not one thing can compare to arriving by boat to a country. It is the best way to travel. I will sail my 60 metre yacht all over the globe. I will traverse the Pacific, stopping at all the little islands and having a party with them. It will be awesome.

I am going to be Captain very soon. I will achieve my Master mariner certificate lol no I won't. It is over! There will be certificates awarded to people from the end of the year lol just kidding. It should be that way. Just like in the days of yore.

Carndonagh is a little farmer town in Inishowen, Donegal. It is the scene of a lot of drinking, just like Moville. It will be famous for tourists along with Greencastle. I have a lot of friends in all three places. I will not forget them when I am living in the South of France and the Caribbean.

The Caribbean is a little 3rd worldy for Con BUT we can guarantee him that he will adore the place when he is living there on and off for a year or two. It is so cool there. It is so exotic!!! A Donegal man with a penchant for all things wild lol that's our Con alright!!!

We have written so many books about Con. None of them can compare to what you are about to read.

About Pachsion. This world is so unbelievably, undeniably lusted after by everybody that hears about it. Imagine eternal life? It is so cool. We do not worry about dying at all. Neither does Con now. There is going to be lots of people claiming that aliens talk to them as well. We know this because we know the future! Pachsion is the favourite of all aliens who visit us in their spaceships. That is no joke. We have a space centre orbiting our planet. People travel up to the space centre and dock with their vessels. It is very like going to sea. Con has had so many adventures. This adventure we embarking on with him is the greatest he has ever been on! Pachsion is his homeworld. He has never seen it. Only in his dreams. We can talk to him in his dreams as well. It is so erotic for us. He has sex dreams all the time lol horny fucker. Gotta, his wife here on Pachsion does not get jealous of his sexual antics here on earth. She is so horny for him!

We are going to have Disneyland in every country on the planet. It will be a mecca for children everywhere. They will enjoy their childhood immensely. There will be no word of abuse of kids anymore. Paedophilia will not be a thing ever again. Children are sexually curious.

Everybody on earth will have multiple partners. There will be a mixing of the races. Everybody will indulge in sexual fantasies. The earth will eventually all be one colour. There will be so much multi-racial sex going on that children and adults will no longer care about the colour of their skin. It is about time.

Only adults will engage in sexual fantasies.

There will be enough money in the world for everybody.

I will supersede all governments and heads of state which are now in place. There will be only one government for the entire planet. I will pick them.

It will be the most peaceful planet ever.

I am going to encourage all nudist colonies. People will no longer be embarrassed about their nakedness.

If people are nude, it will be an inadvertent ballsology to the mainstream lol does that confuse you?

I am going to be the voice of reason on this planet. All people will bow to me lol just kidding. We will have fun.

There is going to be a new type of language on this earth lol I'm only joking. The language spoken on every person's tongue will be England i.e. English. That will be the only language spoken. People will travel so easily then. Think how easy it will be to communicate with each other.

There will be only one currency as well. It will be the dollar. The dollar will be the only currency on all countries.

I've got a hankering for some women to be a sensitive homecoming to me. I have been locked up in a mental asylum again. That is the last time. We aliens organised for Con to go back in one more time. He now has a different Doctor. The new Doctor is an old doctor from his past. She said he had Schizo effective disorder because he could communicate with the dead. It is ludicrous! Of course, he can communicate with the dead. He is an alien. We can talk to every living being, dead or alive, on the planet.

There is a new type of people coming to visit earth in a few short years time. They will be the most sought after genes on the planet. We plan to mix the aliens with earthlings genes. There will be no more cancer. The biggest killer on the planet. Con's mother done her part in helping people make the transition from being alive to dying. It is one tough job!! She is a psychiatric nurse lol no she's not. She is a real nurse, not a medication dispensary.

There will not be a long wait for Con to be a trillionaire. This book is going to sell 7 billion. People who are not English speaking will learn English just to read it. We are an alien race. This is us communicating from the far side of the universe. Exciting, eh?!!

There will not be a very new time to be alive. It will be the most riveting experience for the dead to be part of the living again. All people with the gift of being able to speak with the dead will use their ability for the greater good. There will be no more murders on earth. People will have no reason to do this. So, the gift will be used to help with grief. Con does not miss his father one little bit. His father communicates with him 24/7. He was a little peeved at his untimely demise. He was a proper cunt to Con! But that is all in the past now! They have moved on!

I want to allow paedophilia. It will be so exciting for young girls and boys to have their first sexual experience with an experienced adult. They will not force entry on young girls. There will be no buggering of young boys or any homosexual encounters at all. It is disgusting. We do not like it one little bit. Men are not meant to have anal sex!!! And women enjoy anal sex because they like men to have the power over them. It feels painful but is delicately dealt with by experienced men like Con. Some women like to stop their men from penetrating just before they ejaculate. It is not done women. Let them cum! It is not very nice to stop the flow!!! Men can deal with the faeces no worries.

We are going to revolutionize earths lifeforce. It will be a God send lol God does not exist. He was invented. As were all the Sun gods and wind gods and every other type of god you fucking animals came up with lol just kidding. You are still primitive. That will change inexorably.

There is going to be a new faeces on everybody's face when CON takes the reigns!

We are going to be the greatest thing that ever hit earth. Much better than the meteor that extinguished the Dinosaurs lol.

There is going to be a new world government like no other. It will have men and women from their respective professions in charge of the world. They will have a dedicated interest because that is their experience of the earth. I will let them be uniquely in control of their designated area.

As much as Con is interested in writing another book, this book is not exciting enough for him. It will get much better the further into it he gets. We will be talking about life around the universe.

The mental health of the earth is a shambles. Con now has a new Doctor as we've said and it is going to be another hard slog with her to prove his innocence of all things mental lol. We know he is not mentally ill. The Doctors of earth are on a very slim convergence with no life at all. We are going to obliterate their belief in Big Pharmaceuticals. They spend two years training from what we know to train as medication dispensaries. It is ridiculous. Con is back on the injection that stops him ejaculating and if you have read iCon, you will know how much he enjoys sex! There is going to be a complete overhaul of all psychiatry. They will concentrate on talking to the patients if they wish to be part of mental health. I would say a lot of them will continue with their GP status. Not many of them are suited to counselling!

There will be a certain amount of narcotics illegal but we will tell you which ones in the future. At present, all narcotics will be legal for the foreseeable future. There are dangerous narcotics out there but we know people will be happy with what we legalise. The legal drugs will be Marijuana, Cocaine, LSD and Ecstasy. Magic mushrooms will also be legal. Ayahuasca and other natural drugs will also be legal. This is music to Con's ears. There are a lot of drugs he still hasn't tried! Heroin will also be legal. Not many people will indulge in it. It is the danger that attracts people to it. A good joint is much more satisfying. In our opinion.

As well as drugs, cigarettes will be illegal. They kill too many people on earth. Cancer is definitely caused by smoking cigarettes SO we will be making it defunct. No more tabaco plants. This will be music to a lot of peoples ears. Con included. He is going off cigarettes next week. The date is 14/02/2023. He is making a concerted effort and we know he will do this. His plan is to be able to run a 5 kilometre run by the end of July. We think that is well within his capabilities.

There will be a new catharsis of power on the earth. It will be a new beginning for everybody.

It is going to be a new existence of humans on earth. They will not know the devastation that has ravaged the world up until now. They will read about it in history books. Everybody on earth will read the same history. There will be no propaganda. The truth will be told. All museums will have the history of their country. There will not be artefacts stolen from other countries like the British are famous for doing.

We as Irish aliens are oppressed before we even set foot on your soil. We have watched with an energetic admiration as the I.R.A fought with undying love for their people. It has been gruesome and lots of innocent people have died BUT we do not have as much condolences for human life as religion has placed on it. Millions of people die of starvation and not a single thing is put up in their honour. It is propaganda!

There is going to be a ready made grave for people who do not adhere to our rules. It will not be that difficult to stick to them but there are always people who will flaunt them. Con is wondering will people allow this new century to begin? We are telling him, we know the future. This has already happened. It boggles his mind BUT it makes him smile at how intelligent we are. He enjoys intelligence.

If you have any worries so far of our intentions, please be sure and kiss our little hiney! We are just kidding. Be aware that our intentions are complete of all insurances from other worlds. We have done this in other parts of the Galaxy. We know exactly what we are doing.

If you are already a millionaire or billionaire, you have no worries about losing your money. We were just kidding about sharing your money out. You will keep it! And probably make more. There will be no discrimination against people from wealth. Con comes from a well to do background. His father was a professional ship handler (driver) and his mother was a professional nurse (as they all are apart from psychiatric nurses, that's a gimmick!). Con aspired to be an actor when he was 23 years old. His father and he were on the bridge of a Chinese cargo ship, a rather large one, about 30,000 ton, and his father said to him in the dark and glare of the ships lighting, "this is where it's at!!!" Meaning this is where it is all happening! Con knew he wanted more from his life when his father said this to him. It had become stale at this stage. He had been up and down the river umpteen times with his father through his life and he knew he did not want to be a pilot. He wanted fame and millions of dollars to live his high-octane life. He is most definitely an adrenaline junkie.

James, his brother, is carrying on the family tradition of being a ships pilot. We know he would rather be on stage singing his heart out! He is going to be a famous singer when con takes his position as ruler of earth. Con still can't believe this, even as he writes it. He is not an ego-centric human being. He learned this at a young age when one of his female class mates (they were about 8 years of age! Shows you how advanced he was!!) said to him…"You have such a big head!!" His reply was very humourous…he said in reply "I have to, to match this body!!!" He was flippant but he took the jab from Catriona under consideration and thought "I can't let all this attention go to my head…people won't like me!" He was very popular at school. Right up until he left at 18.

Con will be the most valued member of the famous elite on the planet. He will have numerous girlfriends and fuckbuddies. This is not a bad thing!! People should follow suit! He will also have quite a few children and never mind what Prince Harry says about being a young dad…you can have children at any age when you're a man. Con will be having children in his 80's. He is going to create a dynasty. His children will have all sorts of mothers from all over the world. His home will be filled with the most exotic of influences from all around the globe! This is great news to Con!

People who do not like us taking over from religion will have a hard time finding balance in this new world. They will be of the older generation. We know this already. Young people are ready for something like this to happen. They are excited by aliens. Who isn't?

Americans are probably the most excitable people on the planet! We love this about them. They love their country but they must get used to not relying on war to excite them. All military personnel will be police in all the towns and cities of the planet. They will be stationed with a handsome amount of money as their wage. We are only joking but that was one of Con's ideas. It's not a bad idea BUT there will be no need for any police at all. Everybody will live in harmony. It will be idyllic!

Everybody who has a problem with sharing their men and women with other men and women will just have to get over it! It is a new dawn.

There is going to be no alcohol lol just kidding. Imagine and Irishman saying that about a new planet. It's like an Englishman saying he is wrong lol just kidding.

The Queen of England is the last queen that will ever be in power. Music to a lot of people's ears I can bet!

The Oligarchy of the SoF will be inundated with begging letters to get on Superyachts when Con takes control of it. There will be time for time rotation of crew. 2 months on 2 months off with full pay including repatriation i.e. flights, food, taxi's etc. That is how things are dealt with in the Merchant Navy i.e. Commercial world (as the yachties call it!).

The Merchant Navy and Superyachting will align. All the Navigational certificates and Engineering certificates will be the same across the board. People will be able to work in both with equal measure. The wages will be 3 times what they are now for both. It is a dangerous job being at sea and the pay will be representative of that.

Gregor White is my brothers best buddy from college yet he never gave me a job the whole time I was yachting. I could never figure this out although I think he was worried I'd either take over or get drunk. He was probably right. I don't hold this against him.

My brother Jail bird James as I call him is a GENIUS. I firmly believe he is that smart. He has ascended to the throne in the piloting world. He works in Angola, Africa. So exotic in my head. I loved Africa when I was there. It was only a short couple of months but I intend to visit it again thoroughly. Jail bird James will live in Carrowtrasna for the rest of his life. Not for me. I will be, as I write this thinking of my future, living in the Caribbean with a house in L.A as well.

There is going to be an alien slave for every human lol we jest! There will be no mention of slavery anymore. If you have hired help in your home, they will be paid handsomely. It is not an easy job for people to do. The royal bullshit that is present at the moment on this earth is not how the world will proceed.

There will be an omnipresent God. Again, we jest. God, incase you weren't paying attention, does not exist!!!

There will not be sex before marriage hahaha we like to joke about these stupid laws brought in by the religious freaks of the day. Imagine banning sex?!!! It is the biggest of all jokes that the religious people have going. Con makes a joke of it in iCon, on the back cover. Those placards were in protest. 'Bipolar nothing' means it doesn't exist.

I will always be human to the people of earth…cut me and I will bleed. I am of human parents but my mind is that of an alien. I am the smartest person on the planet. Con still doubts this but he will see his prowess in the future.

Con is getting tired writing BUT he does not want to stop. It intrigues him what we are coming out with. We think he needs some wine. We are going to recommend he ask his next door neighbour to take him in a taxi to the local big supermarket and get some lubrication for his genius grey matter. Go Con! Get that wine!!! Thanks iCon lol Pachsion I mean. Thanks for thinking of me lol.

Wine bought and some consumed lol.

Albeit a South African wine. Not as tasty as the Australian wine I bought a few days ago. Still good though.

There is going to be a new type of money on earth. It will all be plastic, no it won't. There will always be need for cash. The black market will always exist. We know this. Tax will not be paid on everything. This includes working for cash in hand. We will not stop this. It is pointless. The tax should be stopped immediately. There should be people allowed to work for the dollar they are given.

If there is ever a good time to extradite Con, it is now! We are only joking. This is to jolt him back into reality. He has been in a drunken stupor for years lol this we are not joking about. Oh yes, we are. He likes to jest as well.

If there is one thing which we can't abide by it's the misuse of medication in the psychiatric world. Con was forced to take medication on his last admission, then, because they thought he was too edgy, they upped his medication again. It was ridiculous!

I of all people should know that Italian people are brilliant people. I have met and worked with them. Dean de Servienti is an excellent author whom I worked with on a Superyacht. He was the Chef. I was a Deckhand, sailing well below my rank but I was listening to the advice of an English mate of mine. He was supposed to show me the ropes but it ended up being a drug and drink infused trip lol.

There are never going to be people who listen to all the rules. We do not have many BUT the ones we do have should be listened to very much.

If there is anyone who doesn't believe in us, tough titty! We exist.

Cathal McGuinness is not a bad type of person lol he's a really good guy. My father adored him. I liked him a lot growing up too. He is married to my cousin Catriona whom I always had a crush on, even though she was my cousin. I have lots of good looking cousins. It was fun growing up with them! That's all I have to say!!!

If you at any point feel you have to put this book down, remember where you put it down and pick it up at that exact point. You do not want to miss out on any of it!

I am going to be a zillionaire. The alien race aka Pachsion people have told me I will be this rich!

This book will sell on every online bookstore outlet and will be a resounding success.

There is going to be a different kind of culture when we take the world by storm. That will happen over the next couple of months from the marketing of this book. Everybody in the world will read this book. People will be fanatical about the aliens. Con's poetry will be read in schools. Children will learn to write like him. It is so easy!

There will be a view of the mountains in Sint Maarten for Con lol only joking. He will be looking out at the sea. Just like at home in Donegal where he grew up!

We can guarantee that Con will be an unobtrusive, octogenarian when he has his last child. The wife will be 19 years old. This is quite normal in our world. He will be a good looking, in shape 86 year old. He will not be disgusting apart from his chat lol.

Everytime we stop talking Con says to himself "this is fucking boring the tits off me!"

We cannot explain the divulgence of all information about Con to the mental asylum in Letterkenny by housing first. They promised our identity or our existence and communication with Con would be kept between him and housing first. We are only jesting. They did not tell or he wouldn't have got out of there so soon. He was only in a week.

The next thing we are going to do for Con is make him a millionaire by the end of this year. We promise this. He has his doubts but he does believe we are in contact with him. He has no doubts about this but he has moments were it all seems surreal to him.

We are going to be an incoherent mess when we get to the Caribbean lol so will you know who…Contheman lol just kidding. He will be KING of the island in a few days time after arrival lol it will take him a little longer than that. We will not divulge how long it will take him. We don't want to spoil the surprise for him. He will be revered. Not like at home in Rathmullan and Milford where they give him dogs abuse. They are so fucking primitive. They eat their young lol.

If only all books were as easy to write as this one. It flows so easily from our brain.

If all the people buy iCon wildman101 that are going to buy it in the next few years time, then Con will be a billionaire very quickly. We are excited for him!

We do not think everybody on the planet will enjoy iCon wildman101. It is a bit unadulterated filthy divulgence of his sexual conquests AND all the women in it were complicit in their satisfying of Con. It makes him horny to think of all those days.

That was a satisfying wank lol…

We believe that Jail bird James will love his brother Con forever more when he helps him retire and concentrate on his music. He will have his own studio in the grounds of his epic house in Shrove, Donegal.

Catherine, Jail bird James's wife is a school teacher and she is very intelligent. She is also quite beautiful. She will make a great mother. They will have beautiful children and smart too. James is definitely a genius. Just like his older brother.

Derrymen everywhere will stop abusing Con when they meet him in the street. They have little sayings still like "What are you going to do when the books fail?"

Belfast men like Kevin George are going to be an eyesore to Derrymen when Con gives them a million pounds for having his back.

Republicans everywhere will rejuvenate the North of Ireland when there is complete peace.

I am going to be a really sound leader of the people of the world.

There is going to be a total eclipse of yachting when I promote my book iCon wildman101 haha no there won't. It will be further and greater than any book about yachting ever. I do not go into the nitty gritty of everyday life onboard BUT I tell what it is like trying to get on them. Some people get very lucky when they are trying to get a job on them AND they end up writing something about their experiences. It is quite interesting for anyone who has an interest in yachts but not to the layman. I mean no disrespect in the term layman but for those of you who have never ventured further than the city limits, yachting is in orbit!

Merchant Navy boyos will have a brilliant reputation in yachting by the time I am finished amalgamating Superyachting and the Commercial world. There will be a cross-pollination of experience. It will be fantastic. Something for your kids to aspire to.

Bill Kavanagh of the National Maritime College Ireland is one fantastic individual. He is responsible for me going to sea.

I am going to celebrate my life at sea with another anecdotal book of sea stories in the near future. Con will enjoy writing it. He gets a kick out of wandering his mind and writing down little incandescent tales from the crypt.

We as aliens are going to bring about world peace!

We can only imagine lol we know exactly how it is going to go down with everybody. The world will rejoice. No more crime. No more poverty. No more incandescent tales from the crypt about fictional characters. I think fiction is the biggest waste of time reading. Con has got good taste when it comes to reading material. He enjoys especially Hunter S. Thompson. He was a crazy individual lol Con feels he pales in comparison. BUT we reminded him that his exploits were part of his rise to fame in the underworld. Hunter was a journalist. Con is a reprobate lol and now an author.

When we take over. You will see. Lots of changes.

Now, we are going to end this session at the keyboard for Con with advice that he should crack open the red wine.

That was a bit of a breather lol 2 days off.

I am going to be a bit of a playboy when I'm and rich and famous. I have no doubt this will be met with some obstruction. People always like to get involved when other people are not like normal people, if you catch my drift? Lol.

I believe we can overcome anything we put our minds to. This includes depression. It is not a disease like the pharmaceutical companies have Doctors telling patients. It is a state of mind.

There will not be a cover of any music anymore when artists are recording their music. It will all be original.

All movies will be about real life. There are millions of stories worthy of Hollywood star treatment. There will not be much exaggeration. Jesus that new Tom Cruise movie Top Gun Maverick was the biggest adrenaline boost any movie has given me in years but it was so exaggerated.

All radio will be tuned to our station on Pachsion lol just kidding. I think you would've picked it up before now!

We do believe this book will interest the entire planet but there is a little spirit bugging Con. She says she is his daughter that died in the womb. We do not believe it for a second because we know it is not true. It is a Bumbleweed that committed suicide years ago in Moville. She is annoying the fuck out of Con! We will get rid of her, do not worry! This book will entertain Con as well.

We are understanding the process of mental health more and more with every admission Con has. He is nearly at 30 admissions in 18 years. It is fucking incredible. The patience he has had with these fucking retarded nurses and Doctors and the abuse he has had to suffer at the hands of the dastardly I.R.B (Irish Republican Brotherhood). They have been ridiculing him about his weight which he doesn't give a shit about because we have told him he will be thin by the end of the year. He will run the 5k everyday and enjoy it. A half an hour's jog everyday will suit him down to the ground.

Our lives on Pachsion revolve around family and friends. There are 100 billion souls on Pachsion and there are thousands of astronauts. They will be coming to earth to visit in the very near future. It will be the most exciting time in human history. This has nothing to do with the above statement but we had to tweak Con's interest. He's getting bored of all the mental illness shit.

If there has ever been a playboy from Donegal like Con, we have never heard of him. There hasn't been. He will be the most famous Donegal playboy ever!

If I have ever heard of any princesses needing a sex change, I would offer them some advice. Do not call yourselves a prince. They are well over-rated. Just look at Harry. Just kidding. Or am I?

William of Orange is not a friend of the Irish. He caused all that marching the orange order are at down the republican streets. It is long overdue cancellation.

We don't want to start into the nitty gritty of our policies just yet. We are keeping it light! Con is bored to effing tears writing this. It is not like anything he has written before. We are not keeping him sober doing this. He can drink some wine if he wants but it is making him feel sick. We just had a brainwave. Go get some beer!!

All beer got. The Irish Navy were in the pub when I went over…

I've got a hankering for some weed. It will have to wait until I get to the Caribbean.

I have a hankering for some Cocaine as well. Also have to wait until the Caribbean.

It will be Christmas 2023 before Con is a millionaire. This is news to him and he just said very good news at that!

Back to the story…I've been away from the keyboard for a little while. My brain was waterlogged with alcohol. Fucking scary as shit!

I'm aware that not everybody is going to like these new laws but they can go and take a long running jump off a short pier.

I am only happy when I am drunk. This has to change. I have to leave Rathmullan and move to the Caribbean.

I will be so happy living in Sint Maarten on the Caribbean island. All the sun…phew!

And then…all the female tourists yum meee!

I am going to write a few thousand words today to catch up from the last week of taking a breather. I'm excited about it. All the new info…

We are aliens. We are the new driving force of the planet. We can never comprehend how earth is run as it is. How come nobody like con has come along and try to unite the entire world in one common language without brutally enforcing it? England is a beautiful country and the language is sublime. That's from an Irish Republican lol. Now, take heed. We are going to unite Eire and England in one foul swoop. Con will give a radio interview using his laptop. The interviewer will ask the questions and Con will type out the answers then read them out. We will be answering everything from Paedophilia to date rape. A subject very close to Con's penis lol just kidding!

The interviewer will ask whatever he wants. His name will be Louis Theroux. Con likes him! Nothing sexual!

We do not believe that kids less than 2 years old should be subject to sex. This is a law on our world. Anyone breaking that law is subject to castration.

As Con said "we are bang on!!"

Con is so excited writing again but nothing has really tweaked his interest yet. Some of it is close to the bone and he knows it will be met with ridicule but he is willing to put himself out there!

We can take all the heavyweights you got. We got a lad who can beat the whole lot! His name is Constantine!!!

We can take the whole world into the 23rd century in a matter of months. We will do this. We do not have to tax our brains too hard to do this. Con has been thinking along these lines for decades. He always wanted the chance to make these changes and now we are giving it to him. The responsibility is lightly worn on him. He is used to responsibility of this magnitude. Oh yes, he is. He has been responsible for the welfare of yachts, Merchant ships and in his early teenage years a pub. So, we feel he is qualified to lead the human race and oh yeah, we forgot, he is one of us. He is our leader. He is from Pachsion. He is our King. King of the Cosmos!

When we take over there will be no laws surrounding alcohol. It will be readily available for anyone with money. Children will be allowed to consume it but it will be at their parents discretion. Drugs will be the same.

This interest's Con a lot. He feels this is the pivotal thing that will calm humanity down. We can't overstate how much of a leader he is. But there are so many things that need changing. This will only be the light entertainment side of things. Gun control will sort out all the shootings worldwide. There will be no guns manufactured anymore. The guns in people's possession now will be destroyed in due course.

The FBI will not be in a streetwise position to take on the drug world. That will be left to Con and his friends.

All street drugs aka narcotics will be subject to analysis by a police force of our tuition. The people caught selling crapola will be reprimanded with prison for life. It will be that severe. We do not fuck around. Con knows this. We have proven it to him. He will vouch for us. He has had problems with the I.R.A and we have solved his problem. They will be no longer be causing him any grief.

The U.V.F and other protestant paramilitaries will not be forgotten when we are dividing up who sells the drugs. It will be left to the paramilitaries of both sides to bring the drugs into the country. We are not joking. They will work together side by side with the I.R.A.

We are going to explain to Colombian officials that their Cocaine and Marijuana will have to be at certain level of purity. It will not be mixed with gasoline anymore. They will use another agent for the production process. It will be consumable by humans. Cocaine will be a safe drug. It is only a stimulant.

The drug Ecstasy will be produced by the big pharmaceutical corporations. It will be very safe. Ibiza will be the mecca for clubbing again. Con will own the Island. He will be the landlord. Everybody will pay taxes towards him lol it'll be free. He'll be a Zillionaire.

Spain is his favourite country on the planet. The women are very beautiful. We are not messing with this. He is going to have a Spanish girlfriend. That he will call the mother of his children.

We are just about finished for today. This is a very taxing exercise Con is embarking on. It takes a lot of concentration so we are only writing a few thousand words a day.

The last thing we want to say today is "Remember November!" It is a catchphrase by an old client of Con's father's pub years ago. It means remember the regular clientele when its busy and they are trying to get served lol pub goers will understand!!

Back in control of my faculties lol.

All the people on earth will be wealthy individuals by the time we are finished evolutionising earth.

I am so delighted to be in constant communication with the alien race Pachsion. They keep me going every second of the day and night. My dreams are so life like that I wake up and feel like it was real. That goes for the good and bad. The mental health system has left tremendous scars on my psyche. I will never get over the injustices carried out by some of the Doctors and nurses. They are so fucking bossed by my confidence that they feel the need to ridicule and control me.

I am going to have my day.

There is going to be a picture perfection health system. There will be health benefits for everybody. There will be no insurance companies for anything, including, household benefits, car, house, personal body insurance. There will be so much money that people will not need to work but they will be told to work but just take good time off. There will be two people doing what one person does now. So menial jobs will still get done. They will be encouraged with big wages. There will never be poverty on planet earth again.

If you are worried about the earth dying…don't. It will live forever.

There is going to be a massive induction into seagoing personnel. We can see the adventure taking control of young kids. Some children will not be cut out for this style of living. They are not in the way of it. It is not in their blood. Con comes from decades of experience and generations of seafarers. All captains. There are no engineers in the family. Cons young nephew Leo has expressed interest in becoming a Marine engineer. He will be the first in the O'Donnell side of the family. There are Marine engineers on the McLaughlin side of the family. I am proud of that. Even though my mother has poisoned them against me with her whining and complaining about me not taking my medication.

Man, does that make my blood boil. I am not mentally ill.

There is going to be a total control freak who will resist the aliens in every country in the world. We will remedy this with extermination lol no we won't. The people will silence to them.

I am going to be the richest man alive. Sorry I had to stop there for a wank. It concerns me to be non-sexually frustrated at all times. People should learn from this.

I have got to be the most arrogant sailor/soldier on the planet lol no I'm not.

I have got to be the hottest piece of anus on the planet lol no I'm not.

I have got to be the most infidel person on this earth lol I'm definitely not. There will be no infidel talk when we are in control. There will be no Christianity or Muslim or any other religion as we keep saying. Thanks to Con for remembering we already put that in. It shows he's paying attention.

Remember everybody. I Con have not been chosen to lead humanity. This was always going to happen. I am an alien. I have been sent here to do this job and I will do it with aplomb. I can hear what the security forces who have hacked in to my computer from space are saying. They come clearly through in my mind. I just heard "SHUT THAT DOWN!!!" They will not know what hit them when I take control from my island in the Caribbean.

There won't be any more living like a patriot in any countries on earth. It will be one unified earth. Just like Star Trek. Con's favourite television programme.

I am going to be a new age conglomerate. This means a number of different things working together. We are making this book palatable for all ages from 12 and up. Boys and girls will be reading this in their schools and doing assignments on the impact the aliens are going to have on earth. It will be required reading in every school on the planet. Once they hit puberty. They will be sexually active. We do not believe in kids being abused. That has to be stated. Con is very aware that this book will shake the very foundations of every God-fearing nation. We do not care. We have put Con there to rule the planet as we see fit. That includes doing away with all the stupid laws created by intelligent wealthy people to keep the rowdy rambunctious people at bay. These people will not be a problem. We are well aware of these people because of Cons travels. We have been guiding him. Even when he threw himself off a 30 foot drop from a wooden pier into the ocean during a thunderstorm at 3 am. It was a crazy move but he was suicidal. He had a laugh at it when he survived and said to himself "I'm not doing that again!" but he did. He has been at deaths door so many times it is countless. We have protected him.

There is going to be alien fever all over the planet. It will be crazy. Con will live a quiet life in the Caribbean. He will also have a mansion in L.A. Hollywood to be precise. He will work from home but he will also be in movies like he dreamed of. This only the beginning of his life. He has been on many missions. All centred around work and some play too lol.

When Con was last in the Caribbean, one of his crew mates followed him there but his crew mate took centre stage because of his wild personality. He was 10 years older than Con but Con was his superior officer. One night at beach bar nightclub, Con was sitting in the throw's of the delirium tremens or the DT's as its known. Con was feeling very rough. His crew mate was out of his head drunk and dancing on the tables to the crowd. Everybody was cheering him on. He was so excited that he thought he was Con's superior. He came up to Con and started screaming in his face. Screeching "C'MON FELLA!!!" Con jumped up and out of his seat around to where his crew mate was standing and flying back fisted him on the jaw. A move from Taekwon-do. Then he grabbed him by the head and kneed him in the chest. He threw him back while all the crowd were shocked and he screamed at him "COME ON THEN!!!" This raised the ante provisionally for a few seconds. His crew mate calmed down immediately and said "fuck sake Juan! That hurt!!!" Con calmed down and left the bar. So, remember…never undermine your superiors.

I am going to pepper this little book with lots of short anecdotes from my past. They will have morals to them. I have told stories like this my whole life through. I am going to be like Jesus lol. God won't have a look in when I put this book out. The blue rinse brigade as my father called the old folk will bow down and not cause any problems for us.

We are going to be in charge of Yachting and the Merchant Navy. They will be combined. There will be no animosity between them. Con met with great convergence when he was looking for work. That will end.

An anti-extension of AA kind is needed. I do not believe in any addiction. People have a choice. They can take it or leave it. I am aware of alcohol and drug addiction but you can get over it easy enough. A bit of counselling helps a long way. You do not need years of AA. It is a cult. And a higher power does not exist!

Everybody must learn to control themselves with alcohol and drugs. There is no need for laws requiring people to be doing one thing or another. It will all be the same when we are in control. All alcohol and narcotics will be legal and therefore widespread. People will have the choice of whether to indulge or abstain. There will be no peer pressure. It will all be forgotten about in a decade. Kids will grow up with drugs and drink readily available. They will not be subjected pushing or bullying. They probably won't touch them until they start secondary school. After the age of 12. That is a bit young still but kids as we all know will find a curious side to it. Weed is a gateway drug for everybody. It is normally the first drug people try. Then they indoctrinate their loved ones with an alienation of their body, spirit and mind and try other drugs and get labelled mentally ill. It happens all over the world. This is the way of the planet earth. It is about to change forever!!!

I am over the shit that the paranormal are trying to make me believe. They are in my dreams. They make me feel like a no hoper. They are deluded. I live in reality.

I am over everything the local people here in Rathmullan, Donegal are trying to make me believe. They are ridiculing me. Saying things like "washing windows on Oberon!" during a sentence when I'm listening. They can get fucked. They are all going to go to prison. I am going to wear a camera like my mate that I made in Letterkenny mental asylum suggested. I call him Wolfe Toney. Imagine bullying a mental patient. They've been told to keep my spirits low otherwise I'll take over the country. Well compadres it ain't gonna work like I said in iCon wildman101. I'm taking over the world.

Depression can come in waves. I do not believe it is a disease. It is only your emotions playing tricks on you. Other people can cause it. I do know this for a fact. That is what the I.R.A are trying to do to me. Make me permanently depressed. It isn't working. I'm an alien. I do not adhere to the normal rules of society. I'll go get a few tonics at my local hardware store lol no I never. I go to the local supermarket and get some alcohol and that cheers me right up!! And fuck them!!!

I am only visiting this planet. My younger brother got me a t-shirt with this slogan on it when he was about 8 years of age. That was the impact I had on him. He also told my girlfriend of the time that I would end up dead or in a mental asylum. I suppose he wasn't wrong lol.

I would like to express my condolences to the I.R.A at not being able to bring about a united Ireland through their war with the brits lol if you listened to them, you'd think they won. It was brought about through peaceful consideration.

I am only visiting like I have said. This is my final destination. The place I will die will be the Caribbean. I will be not afraid. I go before you. Come follow me. Lol. There's a bit of religion for you.

I am a cocky son of a bitch when I want to be. Tiocfaidh ar la. Up the RA! Lol.

I am going to be a Rockstar poet as well. I will be regaling everyone with my poetry at concerts, at libraries, at schools, at outdoor events like festivals and other places too. I will be like my good friend, the writer extraordinaire and poet himself, the very good John B. McGrath predicted. The best Irish poet that ever existed. I am going to have a wealth of knowledge to draw upon. I've be writing for nearly 30 years and done a lot of living in that time. I know they will strike a chord with everybody who reads them. Even if like most people say…I don't read poetry. I don't really like it. My poems are not your standard type of poetry. They are more visceral. They conjure up imagery that makes you laugh out loud when I want them to.

Now for a poem…just to show you I can do this at the drop of a hat.

Con is the best form of human on the planet(title)

I once was a boy.

Who couldn't perform.

I leaped from my bed one day,

And said this isn't the norm,

My mother's a ho,

And my da is her pimp,

And if I don't watch my way,

I'll end up a blimp,

I took heed of all advice,

All good and all bad,

I left out the shit,

The stuff that made me mad,

I took the good,

And often the rude,

Especially the jokes,

And rude fucking pokes,

I got myself to space,

The final frontier,

I went away to sea,

And had myself a beer,

No beer,

Comes near,

As those warm fresh from the bond,

As long as they were wet,

We could all get fond,

Drunk as skunks,

Sitting on our bunks,

Telling tales,

From Regal sails,

Now, this is a story,

All about how,

My life got flipped,

Turned upside down,

I went into yachting,

The top 1%,

The elite of the elite,

Where all hell is bent,

Into whatever,

shape you want,

And if you don't care,

Just have a jolly old jaunt.

That was most enjoyable. Poetry is my first love. I really love my poetry book 'Anonymous in the town that talks'. Get it on the online bookstore Amazon. Hopefully it will be in schools worldwide by then. Even though there are some nasty ones lol. Children can handle it at 16. It'll be fun for them. Coincide that with my book iCon wildman101 for school leavers to read as well (I'll fix the mistakes and tone it down a little lol I'll add to it if anything. There is some sex stories I'd love to put in hahahahahaha…lol full of haha's for the sex!!! Kids will love it! I can only imagine their essays lol).

Like I said poetry is my first love so here is another.

New title…The Aliens

My alien friends,

From very far away,

Are here to love,

And to play,

They love me forever,

I am their King,

I'm King of the Cosmos,

And I'm all about the bling.

I'm only jesting,

But I love wealth,

I know the salubrious happiness it gives,

And you learn to lady kill with stealth,

Now, this is a tale,

Of rags to riches,

Out with the cunts,

And an end to the bitches,

I'll have some good girls,

With a bad side to them,

But they'll be for me,

So, no one can sue them,

I'll have children,

And lots of wives,

I'll be a King among men,

And a bee with many hives,

I'll have my Queen,

And a few other's too,

We'll sit by the pool,

Smoking weed till we go phew!

Then out with the Cocaine,

Down with the E's,

If anyone has any mushrooms,

To this I will say please!!

This is going to be so much fun,

I'm going to have a blast,

I'll sit in the dark,

And write about my past.

So, out with the confetti,

I'll marry them all,

There'll be no more marriage humans,

But the sex will enthrall.

I'm so delighted to write those little poems they're the first couple of poems I have written to enjoy in years.

Now, for more serious stuff lol just kidding. This book will not be the blueprint for our worldwide take over. We would like you all to be involved but it's not viable.

Another little anecdote from Con. This time one of his sex stories. This happened when he was about 17 years old. He was in a nightclub in Culdaff, Donegal. He was with his posse. He had a big gang of mates growing up. It's so strange for him having nobody now! Anyway, they'd just walked in the door and Con said I'll get the first round. What does everybody want? He took the order and went to the bar. As he was standing there, he noticed an extremely pretty blonde female beside him. He asked her what her name was and her words he will never forget. She said "Don't even think about it. I'm too old for you!" He laughed. And then he asked her how old was she? She said "Put it this way if I was a car, I would have classic insurance!" He laughed and replied quite ingeniously "Sure I'll only ride you once a week!!!" She burst out laughing and said "You have scored!!!" "Do what you're doing, get your pals their drinks and come back to me at this spot!" Con thought this is so bloody cool. He was glad he knew that if you have a classic car insurance you can only by law drive them once a week!! He went to his friends. Gave them their drinks but never said anything about the woman. They had a tendency to ruin things for him. Jealous cunts lol. He went back to the spot and she was waiting. "Where do we go now?" she said. It turns out she was 27. A good Hollywood age. I took her out the back through the emergency door to the picnic bench. It was dark but there was a corner light on the roof. "How about over this?" I said. "What?" she said "…like doggy style?" "Yeah!" I said. "I can't!"

she said "I'm on my period!" "I don't care" I said. She laughed and said "you're bad!". "Fuck it!", "OK" she said. And pulled down her jeans and panties then bent over the picnic bench. She had a great ass on her. It gives Con a horn thinking about it even now. Con got his cock out and started penetrating her doggy style. He was just getting into the swing of it. He was loving not having to worry about getting her pregnant. As he was getting a full steam up there was a loud holler. I looked around and there was the big bouncer whom I knew. The old bouncer laughed and said "C'mon Con ye can't be at that out here!" Con had done it a few times out there. We stopped and pulled our jeans back up. She was laughing. It was a bit of craic. They went inside and had the rest of their night together. After the night was over, they went to the local chip shop. It was packed with people. She started feeling him up. She put her hand down his jeans and started wanking him off in the crowd. He thought no one could see. Suddenly there was a shout from his left. "CON!!!" He looked over and there was his older cousin and all their gang of about 7 or 8 of them sitting down making the wanking signal with their hand and laughing outrageously. The woman was smitten. She wanted to come home with him. But he told her he lived with his parents and he couldn't take her home. She said she didn't mind but he said they would. The next morning Con got up wearing the same top he'd worn the night before. He'd slept in it. He was walking out of his bedroom when his mother spied him in the hallway. "What's that on the front of your shirt? Is that blood?" He laughed into himself, knowing it was period blood! Then, for the first time in his life he admitted to fighting the night before without it being obvious and coming home covered in blood. Which happened quite a few times also. He said he's received a bust nose and wiped it on his shirt. "Ahh!!", "You shouldn't be fighting!" she said. "Yeah I know" he said. He went into the bathroom and had a chuckle. He got changed and so ends the classic car girl tale.

That is one of the best pick-up lines he ever had. He normally tells stories and woo's them. He gets them intrigued and excited with his tales and of course laughing their lovely tits off.

PUA's (pick up artists) will love him. He has an artform of picking up the ladies. It involves humour.

Now for something completely different. All music will be similar. Rock music will be the way to go lol we're just kidding. Music will always be diverse including country music. We hate country music. It's so outdated. People have to move along with the times.

U2 are a very good band. I don't know much of their music. I was never really into them. I just know their hits. Robbie Williams on the other hand I've followed with a will. And Eminem and Oasis.

There is going to be a new kind of regime on the planet. It will include all women and men who have babies. There will be no more taking kids for a walk to sooth them. It is pointless. Too much money is spent on children at that age. It's going to stop. It's a massive western thing. There is no need for all the toys either. A few educational toys will be all they have up until the age of 10. They can learn to ride bicycles at the age of 13 when the bike will last them for years. There is so much commercialism that it drains society. It will all cease to exist.

I have been a victim of abuse by my local taxi driver. He said "I'm out!!!" under his breath then proceeded to gaslight me and constantly getting me to repeat myself. They all do it. "What did you say?" or "Huh?!" It fucking annoys the shite out of me. Anywho, the taxi driver said this to me as I was getting out of the car when we arrived at the supermarket. I was out the door and turning around to close the door after me when he leaned over and said "I've been at sea!!!" It was a derogatory exclamation at me. He was slagging me off.

We are going to not give a flying fuck who we kill when we are in charge. If the gaslighting doesn't stop against Con. There will be deaths.

Shane McElhinney is an idiot. Olivia Doherty wants to suck my cock. She told me up in the hill one time with Shane just out of ear shot. I was taken aback. She said "I suck!!!" and I said nothing. I did not want to get involved with her. She's a skank lol how's that for payback Olivia DHL(Doherty Hor Lover)?

Conor McElhinney is a gay cunt. He tried it on with me when he was steaming drunk. He took his shirt off and crawled over to my chair in his own father's house and started pawing at me. Saying "C'mon!" with a look of lust in his eyes. Fuck you Conor! You can suck my left tit lol.

Cormac McElhinney is the only decent one of the male McElhinney's.

Cian McElhinney turned out really well considering his father is so fucking evil.

I am going to bring about so much change in the world. It will blow your mind. Everybody will be happy. There will be no depression. Everything will be bright and sunny even the rain lol good for Irish people.

I remember when I was little going up the river Foyle with my Dad as he was piloting the large ships. It was not that exciting after a while. I did not really want to be a pilot. I wanted to be an action hero figure in Hollywood. I'm going to have my dream.

Michael Thomas Cavanagh once had a shit during play time out in the grass at the front of the school. I was encouraging him. For this I am sorry. I wonder does he remember it? Lol.

I remember once upon a time on my first few days at school in Greencastle's Drumaweir school having playtime. The boys from our class were trying to find the biggest snail that was hiding underneath the ledge of the perimeter wall of the school at the back. I found the biggest but playtime was nearly over and I was afraid someone would steal it so I took it back into school with me. I hid it in the hand basin in the toilets. Remember I was only 4. I went back into class. I was sitting there when the headmaster, who was to become my nemesis,

Tom Harkin, what an asshole, he was such a bully, comes in and says "who left the snail in the hand basin?" I looked around. And nobody answered. I put up my hand. And he said "Right, you come with me!!" He took me out and said "You are responsible for flooding the whole school!!" The basin tap was left running and the snail had clogged the plug. I looked at the floor. There was water everywhere. I got detention for that lol. My first few days at school. I remember the fear of being in trouble. That soon past. I soon got hardened up to it. I've been so much trouble through my life. It is hard to fathom lol.

I remember one other time I had to pee during lunchtime. I didn't want to ruin playtime by going in to the toilet so I had a giant piss against the prefab building. The next thing I heard was rapid knocking at the window from the other prefab up behind me. I looked around as I was squeezing it as high as I could to impress the other boys and saw Mrs. Doherty knocking on the window lol.

I remember this time I was in secondary school and it was snowing. Everybody was snowball fighting. The vice-principal Wee Phil came out to give out to everyone and stop the snowball fights. He was standing in front of the teacher's staff room. I picked up some snow and condensed it as hard as I could. Then taking aim when he wasn't looking, I threw the snowball at his head. It bounced clean off his forehead lol the other teachers in the staff room started celebrating. I could see them.

I remember this other time when I was in engineering. The teacher Mr. Cramer saw someone hacksawing the metal in the vice up high. It was screeching. He walked over with a welding rod and whipped him over the back with it and said "STOP FUCKING DOING THAT!!" He was my favourite teacher lol. He was good craic.

This one time in band camp I was going to put a flute up my ass lol brings back the memory doesn't it?

I remember one time Kiltboy and his 13 year old daughter Lola were down on the beach. I was drunk and wicked. I got naked and waltzed into the water. Kiltboy went crazy lol Lola was broke in lol.

I remember this gorgeous girl from Canada. She was so beautiful I could speak not speak when I first met her. She ended up sleeping with my friend. He was a badboy so I knew she would like me when she got to know me. I wanted to steal her but I did not want to do the dirt on my mate, Morgan. She came to Ireland to see me. My mother was crazy jealous at the time with my father's new girlfriend. It was hilarious. She started ranting in the car on the way down from Derry when my gorgeous Canadian Princess was in the backseat. I apologised to the Canadian Princess and said "Sorry about my mother." She said "don't worry, your mom just has to get it off her chest!" I was very impressed with her. She was so intelligent.

My friend Morgan cheated on her when she was away on a cruise with her parents. He was such a dickhead. He thought she was boring. I could not believe it. I found her so intriguing. I am going to marry that girl one day. I changed my mind about marriage. It is a good thing to celebrate the coming together of two people BUT I will have other women and she can have other men.

I want to have a lot of children with different wives. They can live in a separate house from my Canadian Princess and I.

I remember when I was drunk and it was the middle of the day in Moville. Leeroy Bumbleweed came to my house and was covered in blood. I told my Canadian Princess and she practically yelled "WHAT DO YOU WANT ME TO DO ABOUT IT?" We were practically married. I could've killed that little cunt Leeroy. But it was my own fault for telling her. She never spoke to me again. I hope she reads this. I'm not involved in any gang. You done the right thing but it broke my heart. I never got over it. It brings a tear to my eye that I did not propose to you on your last night like I was going to. Instead I told you I nearly committed suicide. I thought it was funny as fuck looking back at it. One extreme to the other.

Mathew, your brother was a good man. He has a great sense of humour.

I am going to be an astronaut. In the end. I will be travelling to Pachsion through time and space. I cannot wait. I'm really looking forward to it. It will be an adventure. Through the passion of Pachsion I will be united with my wife Gotta. I haven't met her yet. I look forward to meeting her. She has been in my mind for years. She even wanted me to go gay and try it out. She feels everything I feel. She wanted me to have anal sex. I wouldn't minded trying it but hearing a grown man groaning and grunting as he penetrated me would seriously scar me mentally till death lol.

I am going to have a wicked time when I get to Sint Maarten in the Caribbean. I will be doing drugs and drinking Champagne in my jacuzzi. I will have women all around me. They will be naked with lesbian tendencies. Lol. Such a dreamer I am but I make my dreams come to reality. Learn from them. I will be telling lots of them in the book about my life that I will be writing next. This is going to be the most wicked time to be alive. All the changes that are happening. You will talk about it for centuries. The planet will be at peace.

I am going to be a very avid sports fan lol I could not give a rat's ass about it. It bores me now. There will be no professional sport anywhere. It will all be amateur. Think of the money that's going to be saved. Millions upon millions every single day. It will all go into the fund for universal payment of 1000 dollars a month into your bank account. That will be your lifeline. Everybody on the planet will receive it. It was the King of the Cosmos's idea…Con. He decided after years of social welfare payments that you can never get out of the poverty line on 200 a week. You just drink half of it and alien forbid if you smoke you are screwed.

I am going to make reading the best pastime on the planet. There will be thousands of autobiographies to read. It will be a magnanimous relief to everybody who feels they have a story to tell. Millions will feel it but only a few thousand will be worth your time reading. I am one of them. I have a great story to tell. Especially being an alien. You cannot get more interesting than that as a human.

I am going to have a wonderful time when I get new teeth. I will look a million dollars. It will be perfect for Hollywood. I'm going to be an action hero and do comedy as well. A bit like Mark Wahlberg.

I want to tell you a story now. There was once a little boy who could not keep out of trouble. It was called Con lol he was called Con. There's a bit of gender differentiation. It's fucking ridiculous. It's going to stop. There will be no homosexuality in men. Women are delightful gays. Gay women are the very best a man can have.

I have a cousin Caoimhe and she is gay. Her parents were funny as fuck when they found out. They took her to the local Parish Priest to see if he could exorcise her lol.

There is going to be a certain section of society who this book will be met with revelationship. That means they will take it as gospel lol.

If there is anybody else out there with aliens talking to them it just ghosts. They are not aliens. I am the only alien on the planet.

There will not be a time when you are bored on the planet by the time we are finished. It will be the most exciting place in the universe to live. We can guarantee that.

I will not be subjected to ridicule by any psychiatry. They can get fucked. As Tom Cruise says "IT'S A PSUEDO SCIENCE!!!"

I am always going to be exalted by the alien lovers. They will be in their billions. The people in government right now will hate me. They will all be out of a job. It wears Con down to listen to them on the news. He can not watch the news. There will be no news apart from entertainment industry news on television. If you want news you can look it up on the internet. Television will be so fun to watch when we come to power.

Tom Cruise is a great movie star but his religion is the most ridiculous thing on the planet. Scientology is the biggest horse manure going. I've read some of the books and they are fucking spasticated stupid lol.

If anybody believes in Scientology then this book will not be a very nice thing for you to read. There are too many home truths in it lol. We aliens are so fucking fun that the world will not believe it. The movie PAUL was very close to it. We are not green with little bodies and big heads. That was a fabrication by the media. We are humans as well. We put earthlings on earth. There's a bit of fabrication for you. We are only jesting. You evolved here.

I have a story to tell you that will make your skin crawl. I once caught scabies but I didn't know which girl I caught them off. I was seeing two girls at the one time.

I have only ever done that once.

I am going to be the Casanova of the millennia. I have been so ruthless with my women lol no I haven't. I'm a brilliant lover.

I am going to be a multimillionaire by the time this book comes in.

I am going to be the best friend you could ever have. My books will satisfy millions of people, scientifically speaking lol there's a Scientology dig.

I am going to be the best author on the planet. Everybody will read my books. They will all be made into movies. I am going to be a trillionaire. That makes Con laugh. He is stoney broke at the moment.

There is going to be a vast amount of security forces wishing I was dead. I am laughing my head off at it. There are going to be no security forces anywhere on the planet. It is going to be plane sailing for the rest of mankind.

I believe that the truest people on the planet are the drug takers. They are the coolest people that you can have as a friend. They are so with it.

This book will mark the end of all religion on planet earth. Lol what do you think of that, security forces that are watching me?

I have been so involved with the mental health services that I have lost out on years of writing. My brain was so clogged up with anger and hate. All that has dissipated and disappeared.

There will not be anywhere for lazy people to hide. Everybody on planet earth will be working at something. That was really easy to write said Con. He is getting quicker at typing. He will be a touch typist in no time just like his younger brother Jail bird Ricky lol I mean Jail bird.

Neil lol no I don't. Never mind!

I am not overwhelmed by the I.R.B(Irish Republican Brotherhood. They can get fucked. They are bullies and they will be castrated metaphorically speaking. The I.R.A are close to my heart and have been since I was a grease monkey lol. The Cumann na mban are a bunch of lezzers lol. The I.N.L.A are a bunch of lunatics. I can relate to them very, very, very, very well. Now I must go get some beer!

There is going to be lots of little poems in this book. I will put them in a new poetry book as well.

I am going to have between 3 and 7 wives or squaws as one of the Rathmullan faithful insinuated just a few minutes ago in my local corner shop. They are fucking idiots. Just cause I'm not like them.

I am going to be a go get them type of person every minute of the day when I get to the Caribbean. I will relax in the morning and have some Champagne with orange juice. A nice little pick me up for the afternoon when my work really starts. I'll have some weed then in the evening and maybe a couple of lines of Cocaine just to add a little kick start to the nights festivities which will include a visit to the local establishments.

I am going to be having the time of my life when I get to Sint Maarten.

There is going to be orange juice and Champagne for all my women that aren't pregnant as well. We are going to have a lovely breakfast every single solitary day.

There is bound to be some women out there in the world this life would appeal to, I am counting on it?

There will be lots of sporty women in my life. I love fit bodies. I'm out of shape at the moment because of the hospital admissions. I piled on the weight. 10 or 15 kilos. It's blighted me for years.

I am going to be the happiest multizillionaire on the face of the earth. There are other people that will be as rich. The Saudi's are like that but not when cold fusion comes in, there will be no need for oil anymore. Oh yes there will. I'm only jesting. There will always be a need for oil but the consumption will be negligible compared to now.

There will be so many people doing drugs that the law will wonder what the hell is going on. Weed will explode. Everybody on the planet will be smoking it. There will be Cocaine in the corner shops for sale. Weed will be through a dealer. Oh yes it will. You can have it as much as you want but Cocaine narrows your arteries so take it easy on it. Weed is the best option. Have it in cakes and cookies.

I am going to have an aneurism with all the drinking I do lol no I won't but that's what happened to Miss Polly from the Bully me? Chapter in my book iCon wildman101.

I regularly have dreams about Miss Polly sucking my dick lol no I don't. Pachsion won't be too happy with that line. After all, it's his mother. Lol.

Pachsions father was a Garda and he was a bit of craic. But fucking hell had he a temper on him. Pachsion was beat senseless. No, he wasn't but Velvet was. His younger sister. I used to see the bruises on her. Pachsion said it was his father. I call him Pachsion because he was my best friend growing up and I'm honouring him. He's a good guy and highly intelligent. He done Science in college as well as drinking all the beer in Maynooth lol and shagging all their women. He had 5 on the go at one time. Fucking prolific lol I was proud of him.

I wish to congratulate Pachsion on having children. He will be a great role model for them as long as he stops exaggerating stories. He is terrible for it. His friends all tell him. I used to let it go. I did not want to embarrass him but his friends in Maynooth had had enough of it.

I want to end today with a little beer but my funds will not allow it. It's the first time in a couple of years that I'm short on money. I have done quite well over the last few years.

I was working while drawing the disability. It was hilarious. I'm meant to have Schizophrenia and Schizo effective disorder as well as Bipolar. It's fandabbydozy being mentally ill. So much easier than working for a living. Fucking Jesus does that annoy Con. The lazy cunts could be working instead of sitting drinking beer and smoking drugs.

There will never be mental illness on planet earth after we take control. It is the biggest joke this side of the universe. We have watched for centuries. All these doctors getting together to figure out what people are thinking. It's none of their fucking business. Lol.

There is going to be a worldwide crucifixion of all Jews lol only messing. Just getting them back for Jesus. What a conman he was? The whole place believing he was the son of a God. The Romans ended his bullshit lol.

If the last man on earth was not able to conceive, what the hell would be the point of continuing humanitarian studies with all those women lol. A little joke for the high-brow among you.

I have been warned not to write about John T and the I.R.B by John T from the beachcomber bar, Rathmullan so I'm going to not write anything. Lol.

The beachcomber bar is a very well to do pub. I really enjoy my time there. Apart from the American girl who is a fucking bitch to me. Just cause I asked her had she ever had a threesome. I was chatting her up and she reported me to the owner John T. Fucking what a cunt. She nearly got me barred.

Back to the story. I wish to condemn the I.R.A for killing so many people lol no I don't. It was a war!

The U.V.F are a bunch of fucking thugs.

I am going to learn snowboarding so well. I love it. It is brilliant. Much better then skiing. So much easier as well. I learned it on the slopes of Limone in the Italian Alps.

I am going to have my wicked way with all the lovely female tourists in Rathmullan next year. Oh no I won't. I won't be here. I'll be in the Caribbean living a full life and not worried about the cold at night and wearing my clothes to bed. They stink. Ah so fucking what. They're slagging me off here for having body odour. I couldn't give a rat's ass until I smell it myself. Then I know I need to change. But a little body odour is not a problem. People are too clean cut these days. They should learn to relax a little.

I am going to have as many little children as humanly possible lol no I'm not. I am going to have about 5 or 6. That will be enough to keep my empire going for eternity. My forefathers will not be forgotten. Niall of the nine hostages will be my first born males name. Oh no it won't. It will be something memorable like Constantine. Maybe...ah ha I'm not giving it away.

If for any reason I die before this book comes out. Then it will be over. The earth will remain in turmoil and I will be living the Kings life on Pachsion a little pissed off I could not help earth before I left. This is really happening people. I know you're listening in.

There will never be another Monarchy like the British one.

I am so pissed off at having to go through the mental health system but I realise now it was necessary to see what a load of bullshit it really is. Psychiatric nursing is a fucking joke. The power they feel is obvious in their treatment of patients. They are all high and mighty the little cunts. Reporting me for being a little edgy just to win points. Fucking dickheads. They will never amount to anything on the outside.

If any of them ever come to Sint Maarten they better watch their backs lol just kidding. Couldn't be doing that. There are a few nice ones as well but not many. They all get corrupted.

The Doctors better fucking stay away. I can't guarantee not doing anything to them lol.

There is going to be an outburst from the people about the treatment of the patients all over the world. There will not be a revolution. It will not be an evolution. It will be religious ecstasy lol just kidding. It will be an evolution.

It is going to be the best bloody time ever to be alive. The changes that we are going to make will outshine anything that has ever happened in humanity.

There will not be mental asylums anymore. There is none on Sint Maarten and they are all crazy as fuck lol just kidding Sint Maarten!! Riselle don't take offence. She was really good to me. Even when I broke the sign with my fist. She only charged me 150 bastarding dollars because I got into an argument with a Scottish guy. He was a complete div. No offence Scottish people but he was a complete dickhead. Very unusual for Scottish people. They're normally so dead on. Very like the Irish. Or the ones that aren't gaslighting me anyway. They are complete wastes of space and they can suffer for all I care. They will not be getting 1000 dollars a month forever like the rest of humanity. I will make sure of it. I have a photographic mind. I can remember the faces of all the people who gaslighted me. I will make a point of going through all the Donegal people before I give them the 1000 dollars a week because that is how much I am giving my home county. They deserve it for producing me. Derry as well.

I am going to be the wealthiest man ever to have lived on earth. My money will come from my writing and nothing else. I joked with a friend about being a drug baron but I don't have the patience for something so boring.

There is something in the heir between my brother and I lol another little joke.

I have a wild rover for manys a year…

There is going to be worldwide chaos when we leave this planet lol just kidding. It will run tickety boo. My family will be in control.

I have been through a war with the mental health services. I have won. There will be no medicating me anymore. Tiocfaidh ar la!!!

It is the worst kind of war ever. There is no gratification with killing people. You have to be alert, all the time. They are fucking evil personified. It was been the worst 20 years in the history of mankind but it will all be worth it. If and when the powers that be decide to close their doors. They will have no more customers. America will be great again lol Donald Trump you man you…as the women say when they have a bad streak in them. I've got it loads of times from bad girls lol.

I have been a wild rover for manys a year and I spent all money on whiskey and beer..

I have been through thick and thin with my blonde anorexic girlfriend lol.

There will be a lot of comedy sketches surrounding my contact with Joe Rogan the comedian from the podcast The Joe Rogan experience podcast. He has already started without me. I wonder what his game plan is? I need to be involved. I am the alien of his dreams. I have a sense of humour and I love to party. What more could a body ask for lol?

I am going to be the best fighter on the planet hands down. I will be learning Krav Maga from the experts in Hollywood. It will be brilliant. I will be trained for any eventuality.

If there is anybody who does not like Joe Rogan put up your hands lol just kidding. That's a bit of payback for taking the piss out of me. He has made me out to be a little green man holding a telephone for tweeting him.

I will not be subjected to ridicule by anybody lol just kidding. I'm a comedian. I understand comedy. There has to be a certain amount of piss taking on all fronts.

Joe Rogan will be our point of contact with the greater audience in the world lol I'll have my own fan base by then. Joe's will pale in comparison lol just kidding Joe. You'll have a bigger audience than anybody on the planet. Apart from yours truly lol as my mum from Derry says. It's a Derry expression YOURS TRULY!!! Lol.

I believe that golf is one of the best individual sports on the planet. You can have so much fun on your own. It's a wonderful game and I am quite good at it. I've been playing since I was 10 years of age. That's 34 years. You'd expect me to be a pro by now but years go by without me lifting a club. I miss it!

I am going to be the best singer on the planet lol that would be some feat. There are so many brilliant singers but that is all they are. They are not world leaders. I am a world leader. That is my position in life. Theirs is on stage singing.

Roy Keane is a wonderful human being. I don't know much about him but what I do know is that he inspires people. That is good enough for me.

Alex Ferguson, the Man united football manager created the best football team in the world. I was so impressed that I started supporting them even though I was always a Liverpool fan which is not strictly true. I remember being asked on the school bus which team I supported. I was only about 5 years of age. And my mortal enemy in my class Kidneypunch supported Man united so I picked Liverpool. I actually supported Manchester united. So now I support both the great teams of our day.

I am going to be an avid football fan again lol no I'm not. I have better things to be at than following a football team. I read extensively lol no I don't. I read for entertainment. I like novels that are edgy. I like true fiction. That is a category I just made up because that is what I write because of libel. Lol.

I will never ever understand why paedophiles fancy young children lol oh yes, I do. It's their curious little nature wanting to explore their sexuality at a young age. Adults capitalize on it. And it is frowned upon at the moment. That will not be the case when we are in power. Adults will be able to have sexual relations with kids. But it must be all consensual. No bullying. If a child has a liking to an adult then they can have sex but if there is bullying involved or manipulation then it is the death sentence. So be wary lol kids can change their mind and say they were bullied into it.

I am wary as a human alien of putting the paedophile stuff in this book BUT the aliens Pachsion are assuring me it is the only way to beat the manipulation of children. They must be allowed to explore their sexuality at a young age. I was very sexual as a child. I remember having hardons for girls in my class and rubbing myself but not knowing anything about masturbation. Children will learn masturbation at a young age. It will take away their childlike angst.

All kids will read this book when they are able to read. It will be their first book to read. We are from another world and the first thing a human kid should learn is who is in charge lol that won't go down well with current politicians or world leaders. They will have to bow down to Con. That will be funny as fuck. A homeless guy taking over the world lol. How fantastic!!!

I can still see Riverdances pussy in my mind when I masturbate. It will be with me forever. She was quite the wild thing. Lol and her daughter Angel was a little minx as well. Not bad for a 6 year old. She knows how to flirt. It will stand to her when she gets older lol. Too young for me!!

I am only jesting about Angel. She is a little school girl yum yum as the paedophiles would say lol just carrying on.

I will never set foot in Riverdances abode again no matter how much she wants me. She has her paedophile ways and they are not for me. I was nearly tempted by Angel but Riverdance wanted me to have sexual relations with her son Simon. It was disgusting.

Riverdances paedophile ways are normal where she comes from. They are advanced. I think Riverdance feels this. She had the air of authority about her when she was talking about it with me. I know she likes abuse. She loved me pulling her hair when I fucked her doggy style. She enjoyed the pain. I've had lots of women like this. They often want me to rape them. I have never been so stupid to take them up on it. Fanjita was the only slut that I was tempted to do it to. What a fucking crazy little cunt of a wee girl? She wanted me to re-enact her rape that she faked. She told me she pulled the wool over the Gardai's eyes and got her so-called rapist arrested. It is all in my book iCon wildman101. Buy it!

There will never be another woman like Fanjita in my life. She was a ruthless little cunt.

I have been engaged 3 times. One Fanjita, one Briona and one Flo. All are in the book iCon wildman101.

I am going to go around the world spreading my seed. I will have relations with thousands of women. Lol chance would be a fine thing. We'll see what happens.

I have been a wild man.

There will not be a person alive who doesn't know Constantine O'Donnell. He will be the most famous man ever to have lived and the richest.

I am going to be the most famous man on Sint Maarten. There will be a statue like I said. It will be 7 feet tall with bulging muscles lol and a cock 1 foot long erect and hard as nails lol. People can swing on it.

There is going to be a world shortage of women. All the men will have 3 and 4 wives and lots of children. It will be glorious.

I can only presume that all people will do as we tell them. It will work out for the best if they do.

I can only presume that all people will be as happy as we are on Pachsion. We are only joking with the presumptions. We know the future and it is so bright. We cannot believe it is happening like we expected it to.

Con has pulled out all the stops to make it happen. He is a wonderful inspiration.

I am going to have all the women I want when I'm rich and famous. As you can see it means a lot to me lol.

This book is going to be an eye opener for everybody.

There will never be another Constantine O'Donnell like the one from Shrove.

There is going to be an alcohol limit set on driving cars. It will be 5 pints for a man and 3 pints for a woman lol just kidding. There will be no drink and driving lol just kidding. Of course, there will. Cars will be limited to 30 miles per hour lol how does that go with your human patience lol? I don't think it would go very well.

There is going to be a world window of exploration of the polar ice caps lol there is fuck all to see. It is a test of endurance and that is all it is.

Harry Windsor got frost bite on his cockadoodle doo lol pity it didn't fall off lol just kidding. Me and Harry are going to have a beer together lol just kidding. Meghan wants a fling but I don't think she would be able to keep it a secret when I do my thing on her. It's fantastico!! Just kidding!!!

There will not be any Royal family in any country in the world. It will all be normal people. There will be some famous among them and they will be like royalty but they will not be called princes and princesses or Kings and Queens. They will have normal titles like Mister and Missus. And Miss and Mr.

There will not be a Queen of England anymore. There will only be a down and out King on the dole because he is not qualified to do any other job. What fucking job could he do? Lol.

I am going to be a universal superstar in a literary sense of the word. My books will be read by millions and millions of people all over the galaxy. The aliens will be spreading copies of them all over the universe. Like they did with my first book ANONYMOUS IN A TOWN THAT TALKS. It was a poetry book in which I explain in the foreword that I am bipolar. It was one of the worst mistakes I have ever made in writing a book. I am not bipolar.

I will not be subjected to any slagging off by anybody about being bipolar lol I could not give a rat's ass. The only reason I was annoyed about being called bipolar was because it would affect my work on Superyachts and that is now no longer a problem. I have retired. So, call me anything you want now. I could not give a fuck anymore.

There are so many bipolar people in this world it is unbelievable. All trying to be the smartest of them all. Well my people. I am the smartest. But I am not bipolar. I do not get depression and I sure as hell do not get the elation. I am normal.

There will not be any reason to blackball Con ever again when this book comes out. It will be a testament to how much he loves this planet he has called home for over 40 years.

I am always going to be an alien. I can do whatever humans do but better lol not in everything but writing is my forte. I am going to be the best on the planet. This book will outshine every other book online.

I am writing the memoirs of an alien on this planet. I am going to write everything I can think of that is relevant to my present condition of being a lunatic lol no I'm not but to listen to the Doctors and nurses in Letterkenny unit I am.

I have never been so turned on by anybody as Riverdance. She hit all the right buttons but she was a lunatic lol just kidding. Fanjita turned me on a lot as well. Briona not so much but Flo was a Tiger in bed.

I have had so many women it blows even my mind to think of it. I'm not up in the record blazing echelon of superstars but I've done really well as a normal joe soap.

I am coming around again. These last few paragraphs have been tiresome to write for Con. He was drinking beer last night lol.

I am only going to drink at weekends come April. I am starting my rise to fame. I have 5 stone to lose. It will be a feat and a half to get it all off by Christmas but that is my plan. I will be jogging when I lose 2 stone first. I don't want to hurt my knees or get shin splints. Which happened me before when I was out running and overweight.

I am delighted to be clear headed again. I will be like this until Wednesday. Then I will have some beer again. I am not really bothered about the normal rules of society that dictate you only drink at the weekend. I am a reprobate lol.

I have been to the end of the world in my dreams. I saw an evil tunnel last night with a caged animal inside it. It had fire all around it. I could feel the heat coming from it. It was Kiltboy inside caged like a raving lunatic. Which is what he is at the moment. His neighbours in Paisley are giving him hell. He will not survive unless he calms down. I will try and calm him. It won't be easy.

I have visions in my dreams all the time. Sometimes 3 or 4 in a night if I wake up a few times then go back to sleep. My dream changes and I have another dream.

I have been a sounding board for Kiltboy for the last couple of years. He has a lot of anger in him. I think he just came up the wrong side of life to be honest. Nobody needs to be that bleeding angry all the time.

Kiltboy is an angry little cunt. But an adorable angry little cunt!

I've had the talk with Kiltboy. He has calmed down a lot but he still wants revenge on his neighbour.

We believe that Christy Houston from Derry will not be welcome in Sint Maarten. There's a joke and a half. He became Cons little brother.

All the Derry bullshitters of the day made up stories about Christy and Cons relationship. It was total fabrication. Con just had a dream about it. It was so fucking stupid.

We have only a certain amount of pleasure to go around lol no we don't. Everybody will have pleasure in their lives.

We are going to have a brilliant time playing with all the human emotions. No, we won't. That's what psychiatrists do. They are fucking evil bastards.

Of all the evil I have met in this world on my travels. Psychiatry is the worst I have come across. It is so fucking damned evil it makes a mockery of other evils in the world. I believe when people see the real fucking thing they will gasp in horror. The Scientology people have made DVD's that will circulate throughout the globe when we are in power. They have been very intense in their scrutiny of Psychiatry. It would be a shame if their work was not recognised because of their sham of a religion. They have done some good work in the world but fuck is it a stupid religion. Aren't they all?!! Spirits in the sky dictating. It's fucking fabricated lunacy. We are the only people who are dictating anything. We are the aliens.

Con is up and at'em this morning! Good luck to alcohol lol just kidding. He'll have beer tomorrow.

There is going to be snow forecast here for the next few days. It will be heavy for this part of the world. Not like in America where you get feet upon feet of it but a few inches. Still it brings things here to a standstill.

There is going to be a new kind of order brought into the dating ways of people. If you already have a boyfriend or girlfriend and you are asked out on a date by a better prospect. Go for it! Lol just kidding. You will be able to have both.

I have been to Gibraltar. It was an interesting time. I was going across the border into La Ligne. It is the next town beside Gibraltar on the Spanish side. I got drunk in Gibraltar and woke up in the street at 10 O'Clock in the morning in La Ligne. I was awoken by a guy from Honduras. He bought me some soup which I could not eat so I asked him could he buy me a beer. To which he replied "no problema!" I will be forever indebted to the people who have helped me along the way.

I have been told by my publisher that my book iCon wildman101 will be a great movie.

It has come to my attention that people are starting to believe me that aliens are talking to me. This is wonderful. The most intelligent of them believe me right away. They say "Why not?" "Pourquoi pas?" As they say in French.

I loved French growing up. It was such a cool language but alas we have to get rid of it. English will be the only language spoken on earth in a very short space of time. All the colonies of the countries like Holland, Portugal, Spain and France will all learn to speak England lol there is a little Republican joke I keep using. England instead of English lol I'm only jesting.

I have been a wild sort of man. I have travelled quite extensively on my own. I haven't visited as many countries as I would like to but I will travel more and more each year and write about my experiences as I do them. It will be quite enthralling.

I have got to be the most talked about individual around Donegal. I am quite sure of this. And not always in a good light. They bad mouth me because I do not stick to their idea of society lol fuck them and the horse they rode in on lol just kidding.

There will never be another Achtung baby. I have no idea what the aliens are saying that for. They're obviously big U2 fans. Yes, we are boy lol we call Con boy even tho he is our superior. He doesn't mind one bit!

Cote poets is a little magazine that comes out quarterly in the South of France. I have been published in it. Two of my poems were picked to go in it.

I got reprimanded by nobody for pounding a guy half to death with my head on his face in a Dublin suburb. They were trying to mug me. It went around that he died in hospital from bleeding of the brain. I do not know if this is true or not. I don't really care either way. He deserved it lol.

It has got to be the easiest way to write when you don't have to think about what to write next. The aliens are dictating and I am typing. If only my typing was better. I keep making mistakes and have to go back and correct them. It is really slowing the process down.

I have been in a little altercation in Rathmullan. I won't say which pub but I'm barred from two of them. So, it wasn't Molly's or the white fart!! Lol that's what I call the white harte. They can get fucked if they think I am going back in there. I went to him to find out if I was allowed back in and he lied to my face.

I have just been told by my nurse who gives me the fucking depot injection that Dr.Noir is reading my book. My dastardly plan has worked. I gave her the book and as soon as he heard that it was my book iCon that she was given he said "Give it to me!!!" lol. I can't wait to hear what he thinks of the aliens talking to me. He'll probably want to lock me up again. I'll just tell him it's only a promotional idea. They are not really talking to me lol. That will shut him up.

Doctor Noir is nit picking thru the book. He is doing what the psychologist Emma done. Emma the bone idle cunt said I was like a Shaolin monk with super hero capabilities. Some fucking psychologist.

I have had it up to high doagh with all the crap that surrounds bipolar. Once you get labelled, everything that you do after that is either considered depression or elation. Never bastarding normal. It is a destruction of a human being. Psychiatrists know this and they enjoy the power of having other peoples lives in their hands. And I don't mean responsibility like I had I mean having the power to destroy them. They thrive on it, the fucking cunting backstabbing wankers.

I am going to destroy psychiatry forever. They will no longer be in power of anybody.

I am going to destroy psychiatric nursing. What a joke of a profession that is. Medication dispensaries. That is all they are. Idolizing the fucking weasels of a psychiatrists. The Doctors walk around the asylums like Gods. They are easily entertained.

There has got to be another form of counselling than medication. I know there is lol I'm just joking. Sit and talk about your memories and how they affect you. That is how you unlock all the angst. Writing is a brilliant way to do this. Everybody that thinks they are mentally ill should sit down with a lap top or pen and paper and write what's bothering them down. I know it works. It worked for me and like I say in iCon wildman101, I'm now an author!! That could happen lots of people.

I have been told Tommy Tiernan wants my blood. Well fuck him the useless gobshite!!!

Lol I'm just joking Tommy. You're my kind of guy but you bit me on the forehead last night in a dream lol you were acting the tough guy. It doesn't suit you.

Con has just got more beer. We are signing off for today!!

Not just yet. Con has something that cannot wait until tomorrow incase he forgets. Even though we'll remember lol. Con has a pussy eating method that only works if the women masturbate. They have to be able to imagine sexual fantasies. It gets them off quicker.

I am going to be the most famous sex addict in the world lol.

I've decided to keep on typing for another few hours. I'm bored of sitting just drinking.

I am going to be another type of individual. I'll talk with women all the time. They enthrall me when they are beautiful and have no hang ups. It is very unusual but not in yachting. They are all gorgeous and pretty well kept(I've met a few slack girls!! Hehe sluts'o mine).

I have not been very well received in Rathmullan now the pubs are opened. Like I said I've been barred from two of them. They can get fucked. I'll never be back this way. They can stick their pubs up their hairy holes lol.

I was on the Jeanie Johnston Tallship like I said in iCon wildman101 BUT I walked off in Dingle, County Kerry. I'd had enough of the new English Captain. He wasn't that bad but when I handed him my poem to read, he stuffed it into his back pocket and said I'll read it later then walked over to the side of the boat and stared out to sea. I thought he's plenty of time! I was fucking livid and decided there and then to walk off. It was a crazy fucking decision especially because I was having so much fun there. Lol.

I am going to be the biggest alcoholic in the Caribbean lol that would take some doing. All them yachties. I don't stand a chance. I wouldn't even try.

Everybody wants to be in the movies. It is a fantasy of millions of people.

I am going to be in the movies. The people that fantasise about the movies normally have a lot going on in their lives worth remembering. I am the same. I have so much going on lol no I don't. I am on the disability and there is not a thing wrong with me. I do not feel guilty about this. I'm a survivor and I do what I need to do to survive.

I have been victimised by the I.R.A and the I.R.B and the Cumann na mban and the I.N.L.A and every other Sinn Fein organisation.

It has come to my attention that the I.R.A are not killing anybody any more otherwise I'd be dead. Lol.

It will not be long before I am King of the world.

I have taken it upon myself and also because it is my duty as an alien, to rid the world of all paramilitaries.

I am not joking.

I am self-contained when it comes to keeping secrets lol yes, I am. I do not spill the beans.

I am going to have a wicked girlfriend when I lose my weight. I will be a cuckoo lover. In and out, in and out lol.

I have never been so disappointed as when my father called the police to have me sectioned (put in the mental asylum by law). He went behind my back. There was not a thing wrong with me. It was the worst feeling you can ever imagine. I lost my father that day. We never had the same relationship again. So, listen up you parents who have the power over their children to section them…do not ever do it. You will lose your children forever.

I will never be in a mental asylum again. That is guaranteed by the aliens.

I have not been the best author over the last few years. I should have been writing every bit of free time I had but instead I was drinking. Lol. It was much more fun!!

I will be a better author in future.

I am going to be the pride of Rathmullan in a years time. I will be a famous author and the talking point of all the local people.

I am going to be a ruthless degenerate lol no I'm not.

I will never be without money again!

There will never be another Constantine oh wait I've already said that lol.

I am going to be the pride of my mother lol I'm already her favourite or so she says lol I have my doubts. She will not read iCon wildmana101. She's worried about her blood pressure. That shows how visceral my writing is lol.

Us aliens are from another dimension. We are only joking. We come from the same dimension as earthlings.

There is going to be a world of pain for anybody who crosses us lol another gift is to laugh out loud. We are only joking. There will be no people going against us. We come in peace.

It is early morning and Con has just had his breakfast and it did not involve beer lol just for a change.

We are going to be the favourite of the American people everywhere. They will call out Con's name in their sleep. He will be their saviour.

We have never been so happy as we are right this minute. Con is sober lol just carrying on.

We are big kidders. We love to play around with Con's emotions.

We will only be in Con's life while he is living on earth. He will be a monster laugh on Pachsion when he does his stand-up comedy act. It involves telling his life story. He will do it here on earth too. You will have ring side seats on the internet.

There will not be a Taoiseach in Ireland anymore. There will be a President and he will be the overall guide to the country. Women are not cut out to be in this role. They are emotional beings and will make house for their family. That is the way it is going to be. There will be no more fighting of the genders.

There is no one to blame for my drug taking. I wanted to experiment. I was a late comer to the drug scene so I have only a few stories to tell from it but they were pretty exciting. And I have been doing it for years now so I guess you could say I'm a seasoned professional at it.

I have been around a good bit of the world but there is so much to see. I want to travel extensively.

I am going to purchase a 60 metre Superyacht when I am a Billionaire. This will not take long for I am going to be writing non stop for the next 10 years. There will be dozens of books by us the aliens. We will teach the world how to live a good life and not get fat on commercialism.

There is going to be a complete overhaul of all movies. They will no longer be beautiful and gorgeous. They will be normal people with stupendous acting skills lol. This is not true. People would not go to see them.

I have always been thin when I was young. There is no such thing as middle age spread. You must look after your body all the time.

I have always been a looker. Yes, self-flagellation lol not half as my mother would say. I'm not one bit opposed to self fucking praise.

I will always be good looking. I'm lucky that way. It runs in the family. My children will be gorgeous as well. I will make sure I have beautiful mothers for them.

I have made a plan to lose weight and get fit again. This will be defining moment in my life when I have to go and buy new clothes. I am so looking forward to it. I'm hungry but I am willing to starve myself lol. Needs must!!

I will be fit as a fiddle in a year from now. I guarantee you!

It has become a desperate thing for me to lose all the weight. I am so determined. I have given up smoking and I only drink 12 bottles of beer a week. I drink them on a Wednesday when I get my disability money. I am getting 200 euro a week from my younger brother as well. It is my inheritance. He is the executor of the will and my father in his wisdom has left me 13,000 euro to be dished out as an allowance to make it last a year. I am pretty pleased about this even tho I would like to have gotten the lump sum. I could have paid for the publicity of iCon wildman101 then in one go.

The spirit world are now at peace with me. They hate all the drinking I was doing. They tortured Con to give it up but he was in a different zone to them. He was feeling quite sad about losing his father. He has gotten over that now. Antibes may be getting a visit from him in the coming year. He would love to be mixing it up with all the yachties. He loves it.

I have made a game plan. It is one meal a day plus lots of water. I will eat my meal at 1400hrs. This will be all I eat and drink. I will have a cup of sugary tea and a banana for breakfast. That will be my treat.

I have got to be the luckiest man in the universe. I have aliens and spirits looking out for me. It is a wonderous world we live in. Don't ever let it get you down.

I am going to be a real life lady killer in a matter of months lol I can not wait.

I am really pissed off at Rathmullan house…just kidding. I've never been in it. Not planning to either. I hear it is a bit pretentious lol I don't do pretention lol just kidding. Yachting's full of it. They just want the best service possible and aim to please.

I have been propositioned by the U.V.F to run for government of the North of Ireland lol imagine an English I.R.A man running for government in the U.K lol just carrying on.

I am going to have the most wonderful time picking my wives to be the mothers of my children.

A little poem for you to gander at. It's called my favourite word in the English language…Magniloquence. It's ironic. It means the use of flowery language in a sentence. Do you get it? Lol.

Magniloquence.

Of all the places I've been,

There are none to compare,

With the Caribbean scene,

There are drugs galore,

And drink your fill pubs,

Not like Ireland,

Where they give you the rubs,

You're drinking too fast,

You've had enough,

Fucking hell,

I've had enough,

Up I cough,

With my doagh,

Yet they are not willing,

For me to put on a show,

I want to do my comedy,

And show people a laugh,

But all they want to do,

Is talk about twin calfs,

It beggar's belief,

How insular they are,

When all I have to do,

Is cover my mouth and go far,

Far away to the Caribbean,

Where the drugs are cheap,

And the pussy is warm,

And all around me,

The women will swarm,

I'll be the rich sugar Daddy,

They all want to bed,

And as oft times before,

They'll want to give me head lol just kidding.

Here's another little poem that describes irony.
Irony.

There's an ironic word,

That's called magniloquence,

It's a dandy old word,

And for me there's some poignance,

It can catch you unaware,

If you don't know what it means,

But for me it's so sublime,

I know it means flowery in my dreams,

Words in a sentence,

That cover everything,

From cockadoodle doo,

To every little thing,

That is flowery words in a sentence.

I am prolific when it comes to poetry. It is my forte. I can write them so easily. I read the dictionary from time to time getting words and their meanings. It can help you so much if you listen to everybody that writes. I was told to write every day but I did not listen. I could have a dozen books written by now if I had of listened. So, listen up you authors. Write every single day. Even if it's only a few lines. I know how them hangovers kill lol.

This poem was inspired when I saw Eminem rapping on T.V about 'A thought'. It was a poem of mine. He was slagging me off saying I thought there was a guy coming thru who could beat me. Well Eminem I'm here!

Eminem thought I was taking over.

If I was to take over,

The world of rap,

It would be stupendous,

And none of this aul crap,

There would be big words,

And nothing would do.

I'm going to take over and,

Nothing Eminem can do lol there's a bit of rap for you. Fucking shite rhyming schemes lol just kidding.

I am up to my eyes,

In a new book,

I'm writing about Aliens,

And how they look,

There will be no green men,

There will be only stars,

Of magnitude greater,

Than Jupiter and Mars.

What do you call a bag full of pussys?...Clitoris Allsorts!!

The next poem is a play on the song made famous by my old buddy Daniel O'Donnell, Destination Donegal. The famous Donegal singer and top guy…my cousin as the Gardai in Dingle, County Kerry think lol read iCon wildman101!

Destination Sint Maarten.

I'm going to Sint Maarten,

When I'm a millionaire,

I'll have nobody to bug me,

And nobody to care,

What I do with my time,

Rathmullan you rat bags,

I feel covered in slime,

From all the derogatory comments,

And ifs and buts,

Leave sceptic cuts,

Then I'm about to die,

Of septicaemia,

And acid tongue twats,

They can get fucking fucked,

If they think I'll back down,

I won the legion over,

In France I wear the crown,

They believe in me in yachting,

To there I'll fly in August,

I'll put on my blue suede shoes,

And have a healthy robust,

Of women, wine and song,

What could go wrong,

With the story?

I'm about to collect,

My morning Glory. (Only joking Rathmullan lol!!)

This next poem was inspired by a reading of the dictionary. I read the word and thought it was cool when I read the description.

Leitmotif.

A leitmotif,

For what lies beneath,

From the deaths door,

To wanting to hear more,

A music to tame the beast,

Of oxygen and carbon dioxide,

That is to be released,

A proxy of sound,

An underground roar,

Of lions in heat,

And tigers who've tore,

The music's in shreds,

Little bits here and there,

Worming its way in,

Without a care,

The earworm that is,

A leitmotif,

A song that reminds you,

Of a memory so brief!

The next one is inspired by none other than the rap God himself...

Eminem.

I love your music,

But your attitude is shite,

It keeps me awake at night,

Thinking have I done right?

To take over yachting,

In one fell swoop?

I don't think it bothers you,

I want to recoup.

I know it doesn't bother you,

I feel it in my bones,

I love my little lassie,

She's got a great set of cones,

I think that I am a rapper,

I can dance and I can sing,

I love my little lassie,

She can't wait for me to have bling,

I think that you don't care about the world,

It doesn't really show in your music,

But the alien race are here,

So, don't be going all spastic,

I love my little lassie,

She can't wait for me to arrive,

That's dogs for you,

All I get around Rathmullan is dog poo lol.

This one is going to knock your socks off lol no it won't. It will titillate.

I love nobody lol.

I love nobody,

And nobody loves me,

I act the cunt,

For the whole world to see,

I couldn't give a damn,

I couldn't give a frig,

I'll be who I am,

Until I get big,

Then when I'm big,

I'll act the cunt a little more,

And this will be,

The reaction of the core,

Of my being,

An alien thru and thru,

I can only say this,

I won't be normal,

I'll be abnormally cool,

And sublimely nocturnal,

And never act the fool!!! Lol.

This one was just made up because it has been snowing over the last couple of days.

Cars.

I once had a car,

But it would not go,

I pushed it and pushed it,

But that godammed snow,

Was up to my ears,

Without a breather,

I couldn't see clearly,

Without my receiver,

She was in the front seat,

Taking all the warmth,

I wish to fuck,

She would get of her asshole,

And spread her girth,

Over the back of this car,

And push it along,

Out of this snow,

And sing me a song,

She sings like a Cherokee,

With balls in her throat,

I've got to remind her,

I grew up on a boat.

I know she'll not forgive me,

If I rattle her now,

But I'm so godamn horny,

I'd fuck an ugly sow,

So, what of the cold,

It'll be a nice willy warmer,

I'll get my end away,

And what could be a farmer,

Up over yonder,

He'll give us a tug,

Better than any ride from her,

With hands as sweet as a bug lol just playing around.

We have only been out of touch with Con on one occasion. He asked us the name of his publisher when he was at his brothers wedding. Someone asked him their name and he could not remember. We left him in the lurch. This shook his confidence in us. We are not sorry. We are not his encyclopedia for information. We are only joking. We left him in the lurch because we wanted to show the person asking him how little he pays attention to such details. He is not a maximum kind of person. He is really minimalist. He does not have many belongings. He will travel light and purchase what he needs when he gets where he is going. That will be Sint Maarten.

We are going to have a brilliant time on the island of Sint Maarten with Con. We are really looking forward to it. Lying on the beach in the hot sunshine. So different from Ireland.

We have got to be the funniest people Con has ever met in his life.

There is another funny person in Con's life. He is called Rory Weafer. He is a natural comedian. He is one of a kind. Con's loves him like a brother.

There is going to be a different kind of mentality to racism. There will be no talk of slaves. That is in the past now. We will endeavour to stamp it out but it will take centuries of kids who have good parents and not underprivileged parenting by dim witted people. Unfortunately, everybody can have children. It is not the case on Pachsion. There is a law and you have to pass an exam if you want to have children. There is no room for stupidity where we come from. We stamp it out.

I have never seen such stupid people as the Bumbleweeds. They have a terrible gene pool. They have a shallow end and unfortunately, they all come from it!!

We are going to have a never-ending story. Con is going to be the most prolific author on the planet. He will produce two books per year for the next 10 years then he will retire from writing and enjoy his children.

The books will be a poetry book and a true life story book. There will be no fiction. Con doesn't know where to start with writing a fiction book. It is funny. He only deals in real life.

There is going to be a never-ending story with the drug scene. The music of the day will reflect it. The music will become so much more interesting. Some of the crap that is out there is fucking diabolical. Con fucking hates it. He put on Radio one from the U.K for a couple of days and the depression he felt was all consuming. He could not understand what was wrong with him. He turned off the radio and within a couple of minutes, the depression lifted. He laughed to himself and said fuck the Brits lol no he did not do that!

Con has got to be the fucking luckiest man alive. His life has been so interesting. You will see in the coming years how interesting it has been. He will write everything down from childhood right up to adulthood. He has a photographic memory. We will remind him of all his memories. We know everything about him. All the fun and games he got up to!

Con is going to be a master lover. He will have 3 wives and 2 kids with each woman. They will all be from different countries. We have not told Con yet what countries they will be from. Now we're going to tell him. One will be Australian. They love to party! The next one will be from Spain. They are great with children. The last one will be German. They are so intelligent.

It will be up to Con to go to these countries and meet the women of his dreams. We can not do this for him. He will be looking his best in a year from now. He will get new teeth in a couple of years from now. They will make him look every bit the Hollywood star!

There is going to be a holocaust again lol no there isn't. Adolf Hitler did not get the job done. Lol. We're only kidding!

Jewish people will take centuries to get over the holocaust. We are going to understand nothing of their plight. It happened. Get over it. They moan all the fucking time about it. It is fucking over and done. Get over it. The Irish had a mass genocide called the Great Famine and only a handful of diehards complain about that all the time. It was not that long ago either.

Hollywood will no longer be under Jewish control. They know how to make money but so do we. There is going to be a complete shake down of all the monopolies of the world. There will be none. Everybody will get a fair shot at being wealthy.

We can only presume Con's brother misses him on his trip to the US. Con wanted to go with him but he fucking ignored the message just like he does with nearly every message Con sends him. It is so demoralizing for Con. He wants to be part of his younger brothers life but his younger brother has his head up his ass! The date is 12/03/2023 and his younger brother has gone to Austin, Texas to a music convention to hopefully make some contacts. He has not got a chance in hell of becoming famous in his current situation. A two piece with him and his wife! They are depression personified. At least with his band Springtides with the rest of the band there was a bit of life in his songs but he is singing about having depression now. It is fucking ridiculous. He lives in a dream world if he thinks people will buy into his depression. I believe he married the wrong woman. He was not in love with her. He wanted a laying hen. Someone he thought would be good for him. He did not think of the consequences. Con fucking hates Catherine. She is so up her own ass.

There is going to be a reckoning with the end of the world. There will be no end to the world. It will go on forever. Human race will never be extinct as long as we're in existence. There will be a product of our intervention and it will construe everything that love is on the planet. Do you catch our drift? We are talking about peoples love for the world. People do love this planet but there aren't many of them. Geta Thunberg is one of them. The little autistic girl. Con thought of having sex with her to see what she was like but he decided she would be too frigid. Lol.

There is going to be a worldwide romance story with Con everytime he is in a new town. Even tho he has 3 wives he will still have sexual relations with other women. This is the best possible way for a man to live. It is not the same for a woman. So, don't play the fucking gender card you fucking pains in the asses feminism bullshit artists. Men and women are not fucking equal. Women are the breeders. Men are the inseminators. They must spread their seed. It is in their genes. Women who do this are fucking floosies.

Every man alive is going to be pulling women left right and centre. Cities will be crazy with men all out trying to get their end away. The majority will have to lose weight if they hope to make this their new lifestyle. Con is in the process of making this happen for him. He is going to lose 5 stone this year. So, take encouragement from that. You can do it no matter what weight you are. Just cut out the Carbs. No fizzy drinks. No bread.

Everyone alive is going to hear Con's story. RTE (Radio Telefeis Eireann) the Irish television network are trying to keep him quiet. They will not interview him. It just shows him the power of the mental health services in his country. It is almost as powerful as the Catholic church. Both are coming down with a bang, thump and a wallop.

I have got to be the happiest man alive. I have money. I have a house. I have clothes. And I am about to be the richest man alive! Lol.

There will never be another time in the universe were people have been so in tune with the news. There is nothing but dire fucking reports of lack of money yet look at the wars raging around the world. It is so imbecilic for us to watch. The humans in charge of these wars should be eradicated forever lol just kidding. They should be put in jail. Think of the millions of people suffering because of it.

There is going to be a new world order. We will be in charge of it. There will be another world war if we do not step in. It will be catastrophic. Nuclear weapons will be used. There will be total devastation. We will not let that happen. Nuclear weapons will become defunct. Do not worry. There is going to be another holocaust for the British people. They will all be rounded up and told to sing God save the Queen to the tune of an Irish jig. Con loves that line in the rebel tune Wee Willie John McFadden. Youtube it!

I remember Fanjita always squatting over me in bed after I came in her and squeezing the cum out of her onto my belly. She was disgusting! Read iCon wildman101, you'll get her there.

There will be an outfell of drugs. That is a made up word. It is going to be the word everybody use for the end of crap narcotics. It is getting rid of the poison people put into your drugs and sell it to you. The end of a very dangerous era.

There will be a very long wait for Con to die. It will be about 50 years. He will be King of the world for 47 years. That will be the longest reign of any planet we have encountered. They normally pick a new King every decade. But there is no need for earth to do that. You have our

King for half a century. He will be coming to Pachsion to regain his immortality. He will reign in Pachsion forever. It is so fucking cool. He is so fucking cool! He knows we are serious. He nearly came to us about 17 years ago. We could not stick the pain he was in. He lay down after lighting the fire. The television was broken. He turned off the sitting room light and lay in the floor in front of the fire. He thought I will defragment my brain. The brain is like a computer. I will think every thought out to the end. That way I will clear my mind of this hurt and pain. It worked. He was in a state of transcendental meditation. He did not know this. When his heart lowered enough. We decided he felt like dying. So, we lifted his spirit out of his body. It scared the life out of him. He pulled it back in through sheer will. He did not want to be dead. He felt he had better things coming. We knew it would be 16 years before he would feel happy again. It has been an eventful 15 years. The other year was spent in the asylum. He worked out, he has spent nearly 3 years locked up continuously in mental asylums when you add all the admissions up. It is fucking criminal. Back to the story. His spirit came back into his body. We were taking him to Pachsion without completing his mission. He just said he is glad we left him to complete his mission. That shows what balls he has on him! He was so afraid that he was about to die. He ran into the kitchen and looked in the reflection of the window to see if he was still alive. He could see his spirit lifting out of his body and feel it too. He will feel it again when he dies for real. This time he won't fight it. He will come willingly.

The other women who sleep with him will want babies as well. Con will give them all the babies they want. He will pay for them to be raised and give the women a million dollars to keep them in a good life.

I am the most fulfilled person on the planet. There are very few things I regret doing or not doing. I can honestly say I am a total fulfilled human being.

I am not cock sure of myself. I am confident and have been all my life. There have been years were I was being bullied by my bus shelter friend Con senior lol he was never out of home in his life. He could not imagine the pain he was putting me through. He would not have fucking done it if he had of felt my pain for 1 second. It was the worst bastarding feeling on the planet. I nearly took my own life.

There is about to be a second book in circulation about me. You are reading it. The aliens do not appear that much in iCon wildman101 so don't be buying it expecting to be reading about them. It is just a cameo role lol.

There is a new type of money coming into circulation. It will be the Amero. It will be legal tender in all countries. They will recognise it in China.

There is going to be a never ending story with Con and his women. He will be a modern day Casanova. He will romance thousands of women. He will have hundreds of children. It will be the most prolific outpouring of any man on the planet. He will pour his semen into thousands of women. They will have his babies all around the world. He will be Dad to all of them. He will have an army.

I remember when I was at Carndonagh community school in first year. I was 12 years of age. I studied my heart out for the end of year exams. We were told they had no bearing of what class we got into the following year but I figured differently. I think I was right too. I done really well in nearly all of my 16 subjects (I think it was 16). I guessed that what result we got determined if we got into an honours class. I wanted to be an honours student. I did not want to be in a pass class with all the ruffians. I wanted to do well at school. I loved learning. It gave me a real buzz. I was always on a high after learning something new and being good at remembering things. I learned loads of stuff off verbatim. And churned it out during the exams. Especially languages. They were my favourite. Them and engineering. I got into an honours class. The class was 2D. The honours classes went from 2A down to 2D. 2E was a pass class but we were definitely graded. No question! I got good teachers for second and third year and did well in my Junior Certificate exams for third year. I got 6 B's and 2 D's. One of the B's was a pass level in Irish. It is such a difficult language to learn. I had no interest. I do not think it should be on the curriculum. On any level. If people want to learn it on their own time then so be it but do not force kids to learn it. It is a waste of time. Let it die. We all speak English now. Get over your republican hang ups. The whole world is about to speak English. No more languages in school except English. Peoples English will be fantastic. There will be lots of writers in a few years time. Unfortunately, when I got into fourth year my teachers for the leaving certificate were not that great, in fact, they were shite teachers. I was fucking livid. But there was nothing I could do. I should have dropped to pass on nearly every subject. But I stuck with the honours. I don't know why I did this. Maybe I was embarrassed. Anyway, I fucked my leaving cert exams up and had to return the following year. I had absolutely no interest in sixth year. It was the worst year I had ever spent at school. It was so embarrassing. And I still did honours. I had no help from home. They left me to it all the way through school. They had very little input. My father did ask me did I want to go to a really good school in Derry when I was 15. St. Columbs college. I did not want to leave my friends behind. I was a bit naïve. It took me a minute but I would not leave Carn school. I should have taken his hand off with the offer looking back. I would have excelled. He was right to make me change school. I think he was taking advice from somewhere. But however, it was very, very, very good advice! I often though about it. I did not really regret it that much. I had lost so much interest in school by 17 that I did not think hardly at all about going to college. We had the pub but I knew I did not want to do that forever. It was very, very, very different when you had to make it work in the pub and I knew that. I was only working for my father before that but he often said I would take over from him. He used to say this is all going to be yours one day. I was under pressure all the time. I eventually found my calling and went to sea. That was the life of me. You will read about it in iCon wildman101.

I was always carrying on in school. I was a very rambunctious student. I loved the craic!

I will never forget the words In vino veritas. My English teacher walked in late to class and wrote it on the chalk board. He wrote it in big letters then said In vino veritas…in wine there's truth. It is an old Roman saying. It's latin. Then he walked back out of the class again. He was a bit eccentric. And not a very good teacher at all.

My maths teacher in first year was excellent. His notes were so good that I got very high grades all through that year. I even got 100% in an algebra exam. I was so chuffed!

My engineering teacher was really good as well. I got a good grade for my project. I had to build a crane. And do a write up for it. It was a bit different from all the rest of the subjects. It was a bit more relaxing. I enjoyed it immensely. My father thought I should go on to be an engineer. I thought seriously about this but I had no idea what kind of engineering to go into. I thought Aeronautical engineering sounded good. I was going to do that in college. It gives me the shivers now if I had chosen that life. I fucking hate the idea of working 9 to 5. And weekends off for the rest of your life. I like working non stop for months then having a few months off. That's the way I have lived my life. It has done me proud. I have lots of stories to tell and I have had a good working life. My father told me when I was young and I often heard him quote it. He said FIND A JOB YOU LIKE AND YOU'LL NEVER WORK AGAIN!!! These words rang in my ears when I was doing my cadetship for navigation. I always remembered them. He said that and also, he said IF YOU WERE GOING TO BE A TRAMP, WHY NOT DO IT IN SOMEHWHERE LIKE THE SOUTH OF FRANCE LOL. I did this as well as you will read in iCon wildman101 lol.

I am so relieved my father is dead. We would never have resolved the issue of bipolar. I do not miss him. He is here with me. I can see his translucent(his word to describe what I was seeing when I was trying to explain it to him…he was intrigued!) figure in the air and then I hear his voice in my head when the image enters me. I can feel the energy surge as he completely saturates my body. It is a weird fucking thing but it is a gift that a lot of humans have. They call it schizophrenic but I know different. I am a medium.

Now, back to the aliens. We told Con when he asked why we were not putting more in about the aliens(us!) that we were building up to it. So, here goes. We are nearly half way through the book so we think now is a good time to let you all into our world. We have 3 sun's on Pachsion. There is no night time. We have eternal life. Our serotonin levels are so high from the suns that we live forever. It is not one bit boring. Our bodies regenerate because of the 3 suns. We have no wind worth talking about. Our planet spins but it is so big that it does not have the Coriolis effect. For those of you who do not know what that means. It's the spinning of the earth that creates the wind. Our planet is 100 times the size of earth. We have 100 billion people living there. We only have 3 children per family. That is the law. Earth will introduce this law as well. They will have to. The earth will be too small for the population otherwise. There is too much congestion in the major cities. We will build new towns all over the world and spread the city people out. They can travel to the cities for shopping and nights on the town.

Our world is an old one. It is infinite. We do not know how long it is there. We have no way of telling. We can only guess. Much like the scientists of earth determining the age of earth. It is bullshit what they tell the public. They are guessing. Very like what psychiatrists do with mental patients. They make up a load of professional sounding jargon like nerve endings crashing into one another oh no wait that was my physio but I believe she knew what she was talking about. She is really intelligent. Megan Harding.

I am going to be the favourite of all my slaves lol just kidding. There will never be slaves again on earth. It is over with. There will be people hired to do service work for the more well off but they will be paid handsomely and have great benefits and time off. Two people will do the service work that only one does now.

There is going to be a lot of people asking to come to our world. Your bodies are not evolved enough to survive. We will not be taking anybody to our planet except the overwhelming sensational spirit of Constantine O'Donnell. He is so proud of the O'Donnell name. It's history as Royalty and warriors.

There are many Royal families of origin in Ireland. We as O'Donnell's are the most eminent. We ruled Donegal for a long time. There will be another ruler from the O'Donnell clan. He will be another Red Hugh lol no he will not. He will be my son.

I am going to teach all my children Krav Maga. They will learn it from a young age. They will be able to defend themselves very early on. I know how much this stands to you growing up. I learned how to fight from my father and it was a brilliant thing. I never got into a fight unnecessarily. If I could avoid it I did. That has always been my way. It is what I was taught and I will teach my kids the same ethos. But if trouble comes your way be ready to stand up for yourself. That includes the women. They get in punch ups too. Lol I've seen a few!

I am going to be a wonderful father. I will have many children. They will all be natural leaders. It is in our DNA. It is burned in from centuries of ruling. The O'Donnell's of Carrowtrasna (neighbours of Shrove) are one of the guiding lights of the community. They will always be this way. I am going to tell my younger brother to let his children do martial arts at a young age. Maybe in Derry. They have a great sense of family in Derry. They are great with kids. I always had a good time when I went up there as a child to learn Karate with my father. He was a cool figure in my life. My idol. I did not have many growing up. No-one on T.V could compare to him. He was real life cool!

I have always been a reprobate. I have so many tales to tell of all the trouble I got into growing up. I have my alien side to thank for that. The aliens have told me they wanted to experience all aspects of life. That is why it happened.

I have broken my diet. I got some Weetabix. They hit the spot. I'm incorporating it into my daily intake. A banana and sugary tea for breakfast. A bowl of Weetabix for lunch at 1300hrs and then my evening meal at 1700hrs. Lots of water as well. It won't be long falling off me. The weight that is lol.

I am so distraught at the size of my belly. It has been that way for about 3 years. I have not had the resolve to lose it. I now have the resolve.

There will be a shortage of men who can not be fucking arsed to keep fit for their family. All men will keep themselves trim and in shape when we are in control of the world. There will be so many gyms springing up it will be excellent.

Here's a little poem…it is called Keep fit…

Keep fit.

I am going to,

Keep fit for life,

I am going to,

Find me some wifes,

I will pleasure them and,

They will pleasure me,

With 4 in the bed,

Who cannot be,

Only fucking happy,

And delighted to be alive?

There is going to be a living monument to the alien entity living in my soul. It will be an artist's impression. I will commission an artist to draw and paint my picture. It will be on the front cover of every book I write from then on in.

I will endeavour to portray all the aspects of human existence on the planet. It will be a different kind of quasi-essential portrayal of the class system that the English evolved from. There will be a different new kind of system. There will be no working class. Everybody will learn manners and etiquette. They will not be belligerent.

I am going to have the best kind of life. I will have a jacuzzi room for 6 people. The kids will be loving this. We will have a pool. This sounds like normal life for lots of rich people but to me coming from a middle-class background it is a wicked destiny.

I have so much to talk about. I will not run out of things to say on the Joe Rogan show when he asks me to be on it. I have been primed and ready for this for years. The story of my life is burned into my brain. I will not be forgotten. I will have my say.

There is not one thing wrong with me. I faked the mental illness bipolar. Then I discovered that bipolar doesn't even exist. Neither does schizophrenia. They are bullshit illnesses. The whole of the mental health system is coming down. I along with my alien counterparts will destroy the big pharmaceutical companies and their reign of terror over millions and millions of people. They are brainwashed into believing that they need medication by Doctors. The Doctors get kick backs for promoting a certain kind of drug. In Letterkenny mental asylum. The big drug they use there is Zyprexa. It is a fucking nightmare with weight gain. The nurses make jokes about patients getting fat on it. I've heard them at it. They are fucking going to die a painful death when I get control of the planet. Lol just kidding! But seriously they can fuck away off with their insensitive fucking attitude. They do not care who they hurt. They feel above the patients and they patronize and cajole and gaslight the patients they really don't like. Patients like yours truly.

There is always going to be people who do not like doing what they are told, even by us aliens. They will not be part of society. They will probably end up in prison.

There is now and always going to be a different kind of law for everything. We will be writing new laws for society to adhere to.

The housing first group that look after Con will not be in sole charge of the homeless situation in Ireland. There are other charities out there that have equal stature and have a good measure of society in those realms.

The yachting world will change irrevocably when the aliens take it over using Con. The people involved will all be professional. They will have schooling before setting foot on a boat. There will be strict guidelines to guest interaction. There will be drugs. There will be alcohol and that will not change but the safety element will be so strict. There will be no unnecessary deaths.

There is going to be a world of pain for anyone who stands in Con's way. Lol just kidding!!

I believe that all yachting is going to be overrun by Merchant sailors. They all want the easy life. It is not that easy tho. There are long hours and guest's can be quite demanding. Not all Merchant sailors are equipped to deal with this. But they will adjust. They are very intelligent. They can feel when there is no one in command. Con proved this one night crossing the Atlantic. He was in his bunk and he got a terrible feeling that nobody was looking out the window at the sea. There was someone on watch but he felt they weren't doing their job. He went to the bridge and saw the most unsafe thing you could ever imagine. The watchkeeper was lying down on the couch not looking out the window. He looked at the radars, then looked out the window.

There was nothing for at least 12 miles so he left the idiot to it. He knew he was safe. The idiot looked embarrassed when Con appeared on the bridge. He knew he would pay attention after that. He did not say anything. He did not have to. Con is a Captain. He might not have his papers but he is experienced enough to be one. That is all you need in this world. Experience! No aul papers. Lol you need both but Con has retired now. He has a different calling. Ruling the world! We have been waiting millions of years for his arrival. We have watched him grow. There have been lots of hair raising times but we always knew he would be alright.

There is never going to be another destined ruler. Con is the only one. We know it is going to work. We know the future of earth. It is a fantastic one. There will be a very definite destined ruler of Donegal. Con's son will come home and live here. The octogenarian in Con will not allow him to travel back to the cold and the wet but his son will yearn for it. He will listen to tales from Con about growing up here. Oh no he won't. It wasn't that good. Con had the time of his life in Cork city when he was in college. He could let his republican side out of him. Up the RA!! Lol.

I am an alien. I have been one since arrival on this planet 45 years ago on April the 11th 1978.

My younger sister is thinking about writing a book. It is infectious. My brother will probably write one too if he gets famous. He definitely has an author in him. His writing is very professional. He will write a heart warming story. Not like my sister. Hers will be dark lol. Just kidding. Hers will be good as well. She has a degree in English so she has an advantage over both me and my younger brother.

My mother is an avid reader. Yet she will not read my book iCon wildman101. She is afraid of it.

My father read one of my early manuscripts of iCon wildman101 when I thought I had finished the book. I was going to write a trilogy. I left it on a cliffhanger of arriving home from France after being hounded by gangsters all along the Cote d'Azur, SoF. But my father said when he read it "Is that it?!!!" I said "What do you mean?!!" He said "Is that it? You don't tell how you came alright again in it." I thought about it and was so pissed off that the book wasn't finished. I had to laugh at my father. I really gave him a hard time in it. I said this to him. I said "I didn't mean to give you such a hard time in it but that is what I felt!" He said "Con son, I don't care what you write, I will always love you!" He warmed my heart with that. We had so many father son moments over the years but the mental illness fucking destroyed the very core of our relationship. We could never be as close as we had been. He also said when I asked him what he thought of it as a good read "you should have called in 40 shades of green!" Referring to the book 50 shades of grey. I thought it was quite funny. Much like the time I came home after having the threesome. I arrived on the street outside our house and my father was talking to his brother, my uncle. He asked where I had been? I told him I just had a threesome. His first and only question was "What age were they?" I said "About 35". "Huh!" he said "A combined age of 70!!" I thought you fucking asshole. Trying to ruin it on me. Lol. That was his humour. Pretty intelligent. However, he left my mother for a younger model. He always talked about doing things like that when we had the bar. He used to laugh and joke about it. I think I always knew he wasn't happy in the marriage. My mother has such a ridiculous temper on her. She is impossible to live with on her own. I tried it and I nearly punched her lights out. I never came as close to hitting a woman as I did with her one evening when she was pushing my buttons. She is fucking seriously immature. She had me and my sister very young and never experienced much of the world.

The mental health services fucking despise me. They tried to bully me into taking the depot injection. It is psychotropic medication given every 2 or 3 weeks. They can keep control of you when you are on this because they know you are taking it. We can feel the anger rising in

Con writing this! It fucking grinds his gears as the Kiwi's say. It does more than that tho. It fucking boils his blood into an overflowing mass of detestation.

There will not be any psychotropic medication injections in a few year's time. It will all be over with. There will be no more experimentation on humans with this poison.

I remember one time in college in Cork. Me and a not so friendly acquaintance of mine from my class were on the beer. We were in the Old Oak in Cork city. The girls from Scoozi's were in. One of them was a friend of mine from Donegal. She introduced us to the pack. They were all good looking. One of them really caught my eye. We'll call her Janice. Janice made the move on me. I figured she could tell I was into her. We drank all day. It was a Christmas party. The bouncer who was 6' 7" came over to our table at the end of the night and said "Drink up everybody!", "It's time to leave!!" We all drank up. We were walking out the door. Janice and I when I suddenly realised, I had left my schoolbag at the table inside. We were in the porch way of the door. I said to the bouncer who was ushering us out my schoolbag is inside. "Get it tomorrow!" No, I said. I need it for school. He got fucking irate. I could tell he was drunk. He should not have been doing what he was doing. It turned out he was not working that night but because of his fucking egocentric attitude. He couldn't pass up the opportunity of kicking us all out! The girl Janice said to him (while still in the porch at the front door) "let him in! he needs his bag!!!" The bouncer slapped her on the face and said get out! I fucking flipped and kicked him square on the stomach. He bent over and I grabbed him by both ears. I dragged him outside then swiftly twisted his neck clockwise. He flipped off his feet onto his back on the pavement. I sat on his chest grinning and said "I'm going to enjoy this!!!" I was about to catastrophically rearrange his face. My acquaintance buddy said "Don't fucking do it Con!!!" I said "Fuck him!!!" Suddenly again, a man grabbed me and hollered don't bleeding touch him. And pushed me up against the wall. He said "AN GARDA SIOCHANA!!!" I calmed down and then with a bit of quick thinking so I wouldn't get into trouble said "He hit her!!!" pointing at Janice. "Don't worry!" "We'll deal with him!" "We've had trouble with him before!" He was a big Dutch mongrel lol sorry Jaap! The guards put him in the garda car with one guard either side of him in the back. As they drove away, we were watching to see what would happen. All of a sudden, one of the guards punched him on the head. We could see it in the back window. We all cheered!!! That was it. My GOD was Janice hot for me then!!! We walked home and got to my Donegal girlfriends house. Janice said to my Donegal girlfriend can we take your bed. She said yes! Janice went up and I said just for the craic to make her yearn even more. I'll have a beer first. We walked in to the sitting room while Janice went up to the bed and got naked. My Donegal girlfriend said after 10 minutes "Stop keeping that bloody girl waiting!" I was a little pissed off. I really wanted to shag my Donegal girlfriend but she would have none of it. I'd tried her before. Now, I thought I'll never get with her! Not if I shag one of her friends. I was still a bit naïve on the lady front. I never thought it might help me lol. So, learn from me, take all you can get men! I went up to Janice and got naked too. I got on top of her drunk as hell and said for a laugh "This one's for me!" as I started to shag her quickly. I came in seconds then rolled over and went to sleep. I did not mean too. I was going to shag her again after the first joking shag. But it did not work that way! The next day, I awoke and she was gone. My Donegal girlfriend said to me a few days later "What the fuck did you do on that girl? She fucking hates you!!!" I laughed and told her. She fucking burst out laughing and called me a mean cunt! Janice never spoke to me again. I went to Scoozi's to apologise but she would not even speak to me. Man was she fucking gorgeous.

I remember one time, aka Fanjita came home after a night out on the town. She was so fucking chuffed with herself. I did not know what had got into her. We went to bed and had sex. I even went down on her. As I did, she told me she had shagged Brad Smyth. I nearly lost the fucking plot. She was so disappointed. She thought I would want her more. She thinks that women are like men. Well Fanjita, they are not you fucking skank!!!

This is a poem I will love forever...

Amsterdam

This is a story,

Of when I was bullied,

By my brother in law,

When I was being sullied,

He capitalized on it,

And tore me to shreds,

That fucking idiot,

Left me with the dreads,

I thought I was going to kill him,

He wouldn't stand a chance,

I was going to knife him,

As he pulled a stance,

That being said,

I would not do it,

I'm not that kind of man,

I would not skew it,

I went to Amsterdam,

On a stag do,

I got wasted,

And nearly blew it,

That doesn't rhyme,

But I do not care,

It's meant to be a joke,

And not meant to scare,

These jokes are subliminal,

They take a bit of thinking,

They are kind of real,

Especially if you're drinking,

I am at one now,

With my brother in law,

He can lick my anus,

And say he-haw!!

Now for a Limerick. I met a woman in St. Pat's who taught me how to write them.

A divine love

I'm in love with nobody,

They can all get fucked,

I'm an alien and I'm about to get lucked,

Out of the stratosphere,

Into the earth,

One peace for mankind,

And all of them sucked!!!

There was this one time in Antibes when I scored with a hottie. She was pretty good looking. I took her home to the crew house. Everyone was in bed. I took her to my bed. We had sex all night long. 5 times! I was bursting at the seams before it. All these beautiful women walking around with hardly anything on! All day long! The crew house was full of them but the most I got before that night was a kiss off a gorgeous Swedish doll. Anyway, in the morning, I was just getting ready to enter her again when I thought to myself, this could be it. I could settle for her! I thought to myself, I wonder about her credentials! So, I asked her "are you educated?!" As I did, I heard a roar of laughter. I looked around at the door and there was Wraggamuffin with his phone up recording. He shouted "ARE YOU EDUCATED?!!!" And then took his phone away roaring with laughter. He told me afterwards that it was hilarious. I did not think it was THAT funny but I could see the funny side. Wraggamuffin was a boyo. He did really well with the women and man did he like to party!

I was so infatuated with the Swedish doll that kissed me. Wraggamuffin and I went to the beach with her. Everybody asked me when I got back what she looked like in her bikini? I said unashamedly "She looked seamless. She was beautiful!"

Wraggamuffin was not the wayward type he was a very wayward type. He did nothing but have a good time. Him and Magic, my Polish mate, went spear fishing all the time. They were supposed to be looking for jobs but to everyone, it was more like a holiday. I had a few thousand euro so I was comfortable but I knew it would run out quick. Especially the way I was spending it. Antibes is not that expensive when you knacker drink. That's drinking cheap to you Americans. Knacker's are tinkers or travelling people.

Adam Gilbert was my closest friend there in that crew house. He was a real fucking ladies man. I call him Ditsy in iCon wildman101 to get him back for all the strife he caused me. He was always blackening my name. They called me Irish. I did not mind. I thought it was kind of cool! I did not know that everyone Irish gets called Irish by the Brits. Its fucking stupid. Plus, I lost my name to all the stories about me. When someone told a story about me, they would call me Irish. People would laugh but no one would know it was me they were on about. I was a bit pissed off at that.

I am going to tell the world about yachting. You are meant to keep it between yachties and not tell the outside world about it. They are no longer in control of my life. I can freely talk about it when I am rich and famous. That should be around the time this book comes out!

When I was on Anedigmi, the Captain told me he was leaving me in charge. I thought brilliant. A Captains position, even if it is only for a week. He left and I hit the bottle big time. The whole crew were enjoying themselves as well. I gelled everybody. The Captain wanted rid of all of them. I did not tell them this. They did not know. I thought to myself. They are not a bad crew. The Captain told me to bring in my own people but I thought to myself, I like these guys and gals. The Captain came back and I was summoned to the bridge. He said its always different when you're the Captain. You can't be drinking and partying like the crew men and women. He said I'm sorry but I'm going to have to let you go! He said you're a personable guy. He was full of encouragement but he said you can behave like that maybe once a season, not every bleeding day.

On Kingdom 5KR, I was 3rd Officer. I had a terrible time adjusting to yachting. It was so different from anything I had done at sea plus I was recovering from serious doses of psychotropic medication. It was just after my admission to Sligo mental asylum. You may have read about that in iCon wildman101. I was so fucked from it. I could not joke or be myself. It was only when I drank that I felt the juices flowing in my brain. I could not converse like I can normally. It was so fucking terrible. I toughed it out but I came home because I heard a voice in my head saying "Well you've done it. Time to go home!" I listened to it. I was not worried. The voice said that I had other things to attend to at home. I got home and they were all pleased to see me. I was so fucked off. I was regretting coming home the minute I stepped off the plane. It was only a couple of months away. I was planning to emigrate there if things had worked out for me. I had no money apart from what I earned. I did not care about my family. There were complete fucking assholes to me. They wished me well when I was leaving but I knew they did not want me going anywhere. My father wanted me cooped up in our home house right under his watchful eye! He had converted my Grandfather's house into a fabulous two house semi-detached, complete with conservatories on both sides. Talk about a bit of extravagance! Not fucking needed. He should have kept the money and put it aside for us. He did not need to renovate the house. A good cosmetic make over would have done the trick! My brother god rest him lol he's not dead yet but he will be to me if he doesn't start answering my calls and messages. I won't fucking bother my arse calling him and see how long it takes for him to notice. His bastarding head is up his ass! He never answers when I call. Only occasionally. I am left with nobody with a bit of astuteness to get me out of a jam. My father was always on the end of the line when he was alive, even though we were at odds with the whole bipolar thing. He always looked out for me! I do not have that anymore. I am on my own! I know how an orphan feels. I was abandoned by my family and put into the care of the mental health services. I know this happens quite a lot to poor people but we were millionaires. My father was a Pilot of the river Foyle for nearly 40 years. What the hell he done with the money I'll never know. He did not spend it on me I can tell you. My brother was spoiled rotten even though he turned out kind of ok, if not a little affected by money! My sister saw quite a bit of money from my father. I don't know how much exactly but thousands. I could not believe that my father only left me 13,000 euro. That was the biggest kick in the teeth that I have ever had. He owed me 50,000 to start with. I paid to have the semi-detached finished. Like I said in iCon wildman101, he said "Just give me the money to finish the house, it's going to be yours one day anyway!" I thought why not? It's an investment! Little did I know he would leave it all to my younger brother. I say to him it does not bother me. It bloody well does. But now I'm a millionaire it eases the pain. They can take a running fucking jump if they think I am giving them any money lol just kidding. I will help them out! I'm not greedy. I will help tons of my family and friends out.

I will not be subjected to ridicule by the Real I.R.A. They can get fucked! They have been gaslighting me (abusing me then denying it if challenged. They are a bunch inbred imbeciles. And, they fuck their sisters up the ass!!).

The Provisional I.R.A done me proud by bringing peace to the Island. They fought hard. It was a dirty war! But, they did not try to kill anybody who was not a political target. Accidents happen. The Omagh bombing was orchestrated by a fucking drunk. He was pissed when he gave the order to bomb! That's what I heard through the grapevine. The police ushered everybody down to the target area and not one fuck given. I was told in Letterkenny mental asylum. That's the first time I've repeated it. The aliens are telling me what to write, remember it.

The aliens want to talk a little more about themselves. They are a very unique type of people. They do not drink to oblivion. They do not get addicted to drugs. Any kind of drugs, legal or illegal even though everything is legal on Pachsion. They understand it is so hard to live under the conditions that earth is now living in. People want to escape. They can not do this with hard drugs. They only alleviate the problem for a little while. I want to remedy this. Make peoples live more liveable. I will not be under the control of any government. They will all answer to me!

The American people will love me. They will adopt me right away! I am going to be a wondrous vaccination to their disease. They eat too much. They do not care how much time children spend in front of the television. This will all be stamped out! There is not going to be much in the way of television. It will all be interwoven with the internet.

I will not be a bully. I will be an advocate to the cause of being an alien. Con will not be a human anymore. You will see him as an alien!

There is going to be a different kind of life on planet earth. It will be the new form of living.

There will be a different suggestion of who has the power. It will all not be under the control of thousands of people all over the world. There will be only one ruler. It will be Constantine O'Donnell. He will be known as Contheman! That's his signature. He will practice it now.

I've got it down! It did not take long. It is legible! Not like my other signature…C'O'Donnnell!!! It's been my signature for the last 25 years! I rather like it. It is flash but CONTHEMAN will not be my signature. It is a crap name. I know I got it as a joke. He was being sarcastic and pulling the piss. The guy who gave it to me. He is the only one who called me it! My nickname is Con. My full name is Constantine so iCon wildman101 is another good nickname.

There will never peace if Con does not get control of the world. We will take him back to Pachsion and honour him for trying his very, very, very best that he could do!

I just heard outside my window. A taxi driver who thinks he's a comedian say "The Real are bullying me!…" then he said "Well they'll be killing you soon!" I would like to see them try! It would destabilise the peace process.

Gerry Adams never admits being in the I.R.A. Provo's don't fucking talk about it lol of course they do!

Martin McGuiness always gave me the creeps. Them fucking eyes of his. You just knew he'd killed people.

Sinn fucking Fein are going to be annihilated by me when I'm in control of the world. They are responsible for me being gaslighted. The nurses in the hospital told them how to do it.

I have never been so unharmed as I am right now! The Real I.R.A are trying to intimidate me. They are throwing out death threats.

I have written a poem called Player/Manager. It was poem to Ronan Keating the Boyzone singer. It has got to be the nastiest poem I write in my book Anonymous in the town that talks. It talks about all the boy bands and girl bands singing about things they know nothing about. I did not mean it. It was a judgement when I was heavily medicated.

If I become as wealthy as the aliens are telling me. I will be a comedian forever! I will be on stage everywhere. My shows will sell out!!

There will be a new kind of order in the run of things. What I mean by that is I'll be calling the shots on everything on the planet. It will all run through me. I will work tirelessly to achieve these goals.

There is going to be an alien everywhere on the planet. There are thousands coming to earth in a few short years time. We are going to have the last laugh against the mental health services of Ireland. They will shut their doors. They will not have any customers. Everybody on the island of Eire will be lost and enthralled by Con's story in iCon wildman101. It will have been read by everybody in the country by then. 5 million people.

There is no such thing as stupid people. It is just your exposure to everything.

I remember when I was working on the supply ship William C. Hightower in West Africa. I was Second Officer. The heat was unbelievable. I was on deck and we had an armed soldier as security. He was in his full regalia. It must have been so hot for him. I took pity on him and went and got him a can of Cola. I brought it out and got a deck chair and took it over to him where he was standing at the end of the gangway up to the quay. It was access to the boat. I sat him in the shade underneath the gangway. It was low tide. So, the gangway was at an angle of 70 degrees. It was a few moments later that one of the local hoodlums marched onto the boat and demanded I sell him some paint. I said no. He got angry and said "What you give to me?!!!" I said wait a minute and I picked my nose and held it out for him and said "Here you go! You can have that!!!" He went fucking mental "That is disgusting!!!" he said. He looked like he was going to get violent. The soldier stood up unbeknownst to the hood and put the rifle to his head and cocked the pin. He said "Get off the boat!!!" The guy was fucking so angry. I looked at him and smiled and waved bye bye!

I was so involved with the ladies in Nigeria! They were so sexual. They all wanted sex from us. We thought this was going to be a brilliant time. The wooden canoes came paddling around the bend as we looked up the river. It was early in the day. They pulled up beside our boat and they were all dressed in their best gear. They were saying you want to party? They were keeping us entertained. The skipper of the canoe had an ice box and he said get a bucket and we will pass you up some beer if you pay us. We had plenty of money. We drank well into the night. About 1 O'Clock in the morning, the skipper said you want a lady. I said yeah why not? We put down the ladder and we climbed down to the canoes for the craic. Me and Ryan the 2nd Engineer. We were both pals. The girls were excited. Ryan and I started scooting water at each other. One of the madams got wet. She climbed the ladder in a fit of temper. She got on the ship and started screaming "Get the Captain!!! I want money for new clothes!" I lost my cool with her. I climbed up the ladder. I told her to shut the fuck up. I told her the Captain is in bed. And there was nothing wrong with her. It was only water! She was going berserk! I grabbed her and picked her up in my arms with her legs and arms hanging there. I help her over the side and yelled at her shut the fuck up or I'll drop you! She quietened down.

My father told me that his father told him when he was going away to sea "BE THE SOFT CUNT OR THE HARD PRICK, BUT REMEMBER, THE HARD PRICK FUCKS THE SOFT CUNT EVERY TIME!!!" He told me this when I was going to sea. It stood me well. I have now told my nephew Leo this. He is going to be a Marine Engineer. I'm so delighted for him…

This is a poem by us aliens to cheer Con up that he has to start writing again lol

Las night

I've been to Las Vegas,

I've had a pee,

In the Belagio fountains,

When I was wee,

I was on a Superyacht,

Owned by a Billionaire,

The laugh we had,

Was okay,

But better when you are Galihad.

The story I'm about to relate is a very combustious one. It is about the Greasers in Moville. They are a family of about 20 children and they ruled the town, or tried to rule it as teenagers. They were the DEA as my mate Damo called them. He got two black eyes from them at my 18th birthday party for smoking hash. They were not invited. The story unfolds as I am growing up behind our pub counter, listening to tales of their bullying in the town of Moville. It enraged me so much that nobody would stand up against them. I was too young to do anything. When I hit 18 I started really drinking about the town. One night in McNamara's hotel at a newly opened disco they accosted me. One of their henchmen, not a greaser but a greaser wannabe, put a look into my soul that got fucking accosted back. He said as I walked out last, following our group of men from Shroove, "There's a cunt there I must get!" I looked at him and he was staring out at the dance floor. As I looked at him, he changed his attention to me and said "There's another cunt I must get…" I could tell by the look in his eye that he was trying to intimidate me. It was their usual fucking playtime schoolboy bullying tactics. We've since made up. I said "What do you have to get me for?" He grabbed me by the throat and yelled "Don't talk back to me!!!" I knocked his hand away. Grabbed him by the throat, spun him around and walloped him on the cheekbone with my steelbinded right fist. He went flying o'er a table full of glasses. I lost my cool and screamed at the rest of the gang standing there "C'MON YOU GREASING CUNTS. THERE'S ONLY ONE OF ME!!!" I was looking at the head man… Joe the Greaser. They all said "no trouble." I went to walk out and the bouncer tried putting his arm around me to walk me out. I screamed at him "GET YOUR FILTHY HANDS OFF ME…THERE'S ONE OF ME AND 10 OF THEM AND YOU THROW ME OUT?!!!" I then jumped up and did a scissor kick, kicking the disco front door open and walking out. I met my friend outside. He asked me what happened? I told him. We walked off with me fuming. The next week came and I told my mates that we are going back to that nightclub. I said to them "Them cunts are not intimidating us!!!" We went back the following Saturday night and they were there. My mate Norri said "don't go to the toilet without one of us". I got a little wayward with the sauce and was out dancing with some ladies, forgetting the plan. I went to the toilet and was having a pee when I heard this deep voice say "You marked Alan Diver!". I turned around to see Joe and Ray standing there. I finished my pee and was really glad I brought my bottle of miller with me. I was gonna cut them to pieces if they attacked me. I said "So what? He grabbed me by the throat!" Ray said "That's no reason to hit someone. If a man hits you, you hit him back." "Not in my book" I said. Ray was looking at Joe for a reaction. Joe stared at me wondering what made me tick. I could tell. This wasn't my first Rodeo. Joe said "You better watch your back around this town!!!" I said "In case the fact has escaped you, I don't live in this town. You watch your back!" I was serious but laughing at them. I had a massive gang of old and young that I knew hated them. If they laid a finger on me, I thought, there would be WAR!!! Joe said "No you watch yours. Our father is a very powerful man about this town." I said "I told you I don't live in this town! You think you have a big family? Wait till you see mine! We will come up and BURN YOUR HOUSE OUT!!!" They both went silent. I walked out of the bathroom, leaving them both standing there. As I opened the bathroom door, the other mob of theirs made moves to run in. They were all going to join in on beating me up. The town would have been ransacked until every last one of them was in serious pain. I am not kidding. My Daddy was mental. He went up to their house after this happened. Someone told him I was getting hassle from them. I kept it quiet. I wanted to deal with it myself. It was how I was brought up. Daddy thought otherwise and went into their kitchen unannounced and told them…"Stay away from my son." And walked out the door again. The I.R.A then threatened them in Derry. A gun was put to Ray the Greasers head in a toilet of a pub on the Strand road, The Strand Bar, and he was told "Calm down or you are all kneecapped…" They had no choice but to calm down. Totally unrelated.

The people of Rathmullan are tearing at my soul. They are telling me everyday that the rumours of my alien ancestry is bullshit. They are going to be so fucking in deficit mindful delusions for the rest of humanity when I leave and tell of my time here.

The life I live here in Rathmullan is pretty sheltered. The people living here are very nosey. They are so fucking nosey that they even comment on how many times I go to the chip van to eat in a week. They are so bloody intrusive that they comment on this to each other within earshot of me. They love to brow beat me. It doesn't bloody work people. I'm an alien. I am not human. Con points out here, as we are talking, that there is no difference between us. We are all alien. This is kind of true. The humans on earth have been altered so they do not have the knowledge of their ancestors. Con has this in his DNA. He comes from a long line of Captains. He has the saltwater in his blood. The humans that are living on earth and in Rathmullan are not very intelligent on average. They are worker bees. They live below the normal parameters of intelligence for the likes of a lawyer or Doctor. Things that Con is used to having in his rich industrious life. These people have a brain and can hold a conversation without talking about somebody maliciously or gossipingly.

Today is a good day…I'm 6 months into writing this book and I've only written half of it. The other half is gonna be mind blowing…I'll write it in the next few months. It's a brilliant day because today is the day, I get my disability from the social services and I can buy my wine and beer. I know it is not that big a deal but I never paid taxes lol.

I have been a Soldier of the I.R.A for my whole life. I have completed missions for them. No killing but all political. They have been so high octane. You can read all about them in iCon Wildman101.

It is 12 O'Clock. Just another couple of hours and I can drink my fill of wine of the lovely vintage...Red lol.

Excellent times ahead!!!

BOOK 2 OF 3

Is feidir liom (1 can as Gaelige...)

This a new edition of poetry from the alien race. I have got to be the most interesting new poet on the planet…an alien poet from a different Galaxy.

Con is the best form of human on the planet

I once was a boy.

Who couldn't perform.

I leaped from my bed one day,

And said this isn't the norm,

My mother's a ho,

And my da is her pimp,

And if I don't watch my way,

I'll end up a blimp,

I took heed of all advice,

All good and all bad,

I left out the shit,

The stuff that made me mad,

I took the good,

And often the rude,

Especially the jokes,

And rude fucking pokes,

I got myself to space,

The final frontier,

I went away to sea,

And had myself a beer,

No beer,

Comes near,

As those warm fresh from the bond,

As long as they were wet,

We could all get fond,

Drunk as skunks,

Sitting on our bunks,

Telling tales,

From Regal sails,

Now, this is a story,

All about how,

My life got flipped,

Turned upside down,

I went into yachting,

The top 1%,

The elite of the elite,

Where all hell is bent,

Into whatever,

shape you want,

And if you don't care,

Just have a jolly old jaunt.

The Aliens

My alien friends,

From very far away,

Are here to love,

And to play,

They love me forever,

I am their King,

I'm King of the Cosmos,

And I'm all about the bling.

I'm only jesting,

But I love wealth,

I know the salubrious happiness it gives,

And you learn to lady kill with stealth,

Now, this is a tale,

Of rags to riches,

Out with the cunts,

And an end to the bitches,

I'll have some good girls,

With a bad side to them,

But they'll be for me,

So, no one can sue them,

I'll have children,

And lots of wives,

I'll be a King among men,

And a bee with many hives,

I'll have my Queen,

And a few other's too,

We'll sit by the pool,

Smoking weed till we go phew!

Then out with the Cocaine,

Down with the E's,

If anyone has any mushrooms,

To this I will say please!!

This is going to be so much fun,

I'm going to have a blast,

I'll sit in the dark,

And write about my past.

So, out with the confetti,

I'll marry them all,

There'll be no more marriage humans,

But the sex will enthrall.

A little poem for you to gander at. It's called my favourite word in the English language...Magniloquence. It's ironic. It means the use of flowery language in a sentence. Do you get it? Lol.

Magniloquence

Of all the places I've been,

There are none to compare,

With the Caribbean scene,

There are drugs galore,

And drink your fill pubs,

Not like Ireland,

Where they give you the rubs,

You're drinking too fast,

You've had enough,

Fucking hell,

I've had enough,

Up I cough,

With my doagh,

Yet they are not willing,

For me to put on a show,

I want to do my comedy,

And show people a laugh,

But all they want to do,

Is talk about twin calfs,

It beggar's belief,

How insular they are,

When all I have to do,

Is cover my mouth and go far,

Far away to the Caribbean,

Where the drugs are cheap,

And the pussy is warm,

And all around me,

The women will swarm,

I'll be the rich sugar Daddy,

They all want to bed,

And as oft times before,

They'll want to give me head lol just kidding.

Here's another little poem that describes irony.

Irony

There's an ironic word,

That's called magniloquence,

It's a dandy old word,

And for me there's some poignance,

It can catch you unaware,

If you don't know what it means,

But for me it's so sublime,

I know it means flowery in my dreams,

Words in a sentence,

That cover everything,

From cockadoodle doo,

To every little thing,

That is flowery words in a sentence.

This poem was inspired when I saw Eminem rapping on T.V about 'A thought'. It was a poem of mine. He was slagging me off saying I thought there was a guy coming thru who could beat me. Well Eminem I'm here!

Eminem thought I was taking over

If I was to take over,

The world of rap,

It would be stupendous,

And none of this aul crap,

There would be big words,

And nothing would do.

I'm going to take over and,

Nothing Eminem can do lol there's a bit of rap for you. Fucking shite rhyming schemes lol just kidding.

I am up to my eyes,

In a new book,

I'm writing about Aliens,

And how they look,

There will be no green men,

There will be only stars,

Of magnitude greater,

Than Jupiter and Mars.

What do you call a bag full of pussys?...Clitoris Allsorts!!

The next poem is a play on the song made famous by my old buddy Daniel O'Donnell, Destination Donegal. The famous Donegal singer and top guy…my cousin as the Gardai in Dingle, County Kerry think lol read iCon wildman101!

Destination Sint Maarten

I'm going to Sint Maarten,

When I'm a millionaire,

I'll have nobody to bug me,

And nobody to care,

What I do with my time,

Rathmullan you rat bags,

I feel covered in slime,

From all the derogatory comments,

And ifs and buts,

Leave sceptic cuts,

Then I'm about to die,

Of septicaemia,

And acid tongue twats,

They can get fucking fucked,

If they think I'll back down,

I won the legion over,

In France I wear the crown,

They believe in me in yachting,

To there I'll fly in August,

I'll put on my blue suede shoes,

And have a healthy robust,

Of women, wine and song,

What could go wrong,

With the story?

I'm about to collect,

My morning Glory. (Only joking Rathmullan lol!!)

This next poem was inspired by a reading of the dictionary. I read the word and thought it was cool when I read the description.

Leitmotif

A leitmotif,

For what lies beneath,

From the deaths door,

To wanting to hear more,

A music to tame the beast,

Of oxygen and carbon dioxide,

That is to be released,

A proxy of sound,

An underground roar,

Of lions in heat,

And tigers who've tore,

The music's in shreds,

Little bits here and there,

Worming its way in,

Without a care,

The earworm that is,

A leitmotif,

A song that reminds you,

Of a memory so brief!

The next one is inspired by none other than the rap God himself…

Eminem

I love your music,

But your attitude is shite,

It keeps me awake at night,

Thinking have I done right?

To take over yachting,

In one fell swoop?

I don't think it bothers you,

I want to recoup.

I know it doesn't bother you,

I feel it in my bones,

I love my little lassie,

She's got a great set of cones,

I think that I am a rapper,

I can dance and I can sing,

I love my little lassie,

She can't wait for me to have bling,

I think that you don't care about the world,

It doesn't really show in your music,

But the alien race are here,

So, don't be going all spastic,

I love my little lassie,

She can't wait for me to arrive,

That's dogs for you,

All I get around Rathmullan is dog poo lol.

This one is going to knock your socks off lol no it won't. It will titillate.

I love nobody lol

I love nobody,

And nobody loves me,

I act the cunt,

For the whole world to see,

I couldn't give a damn,

I couldn't give a frig,

I'll be who I am,

Until I get big,

Then when I'm big,

I'll act the cunt a little more,

And this will be,

The reaction of the core,

Of my being,

An alien thru and thru,

I can only say this,

I won't be normal,

I'll be abnormally cool,

And sublimely nocturnal,

And never act the fool!!! Lol.

This one was just made up because it has been snowing over the last couple of days.

Cars

I once had a car,

But it would not go,

I pushed it and pushed it,

But that godammed snow,

Was up to my ears,

Without a breather,

I couldn't see clearly,

Without my receiver,

She was in the front seat,

Taking all the warmth,

I wish to fuck,

She would get off her asshole,

And spread her girth,

Over the back of this car,

And push it along,

Out of this snow,

And sing me a song,

She sings like a Cherokee,

With balls in her throat,

I've got to remind her,

I grew up on a boat.

I know she'll not forgive me,

If I rattle her now,

But I'm so godamn horny,

I'd fuck an ugly sow,

So, what of the cold?

It'll be a nice willy warmer,

I'll get my end away,

And what could be a farmer,

Up over yonder,

He'll give us a tug,

Better than any ride from her,

With hands as sweet as a bug lol just playing around.

Here's a little poem…it is called Keep fit…

Keep fit

I am going to,

Keep fit for life,

I am going to,

Find me some wifes,

I will pleasure them and,

They will pleasure me,

With 4 in the bed,

Who cannot be,

Only fucking happy,

And delighted to be alive?

Amsterdam

This is a story,

Of when I was bullied,

By my brother in law,

When I was being sullied,

He capitalized on it,

And tore me to shreds,

That fucking idiot,

Left me with the dreads,

I thought I was going to kill him,

He wouldn't stand a chance,

I was going to knife him,

As he pulled a stance,

That being said,

I would not do it,

I'm not that kind of man,

I would not skew it,

I went to Amsterdam,

On a stag do,

I got wasted,

And nearly blew it,

That doesn't rhyme,

But I do not care,

It's meant to be a joke,

And not meant to scare,

These jokes are subliminal,

They take a bit of thinking,

They are kind of real,

Especially if you're drinking,

I am at one now,

With my brother in law,

He can lick my anus,

And say he-haw!!

Now for a Limerick. I met a woman in St. Pat's mental asylum who taught me how to write them.

A divine love

I'm in love with nobody,

They can all get fucked,

I'm an alien and I'm about to get lucked,

Out of the stratosphere,

Into the earth,

One peace for mankind,

And all of them sucked!!!

This has got to be the easiest book ever written.

I am loving it

I love love itself,

Lol no I don't.

Love does not exist, it's infatuation,

All love was lost when,

The rifles bleed the soldiers dry,

On the battle fields,

Of the Somme,

This is an ode to the soldiers of,

World war 2,

I don't believe in love,

I believe in happiness,

If you do not believe me,

Get your head examined lol,

That doesn't exist either,

There is no mental illness,

We do not believe in the coultering arms of Phil!

He writes about love and,

So, does everybody who writes songs,

This is a song.

We are going to bring about peace

The love that we feel for the human race,

Can be seen on our face,

It will shed new light upon,

Everything that is iCon,

The love that we are going to spread,

Will leave you wondering why God is dead?

Lol no it won't you'll be happy,

And Con will tell you the story,

About his Dad and the nappy,

He used to hold onto his excrement,

He was having too much fun,

To go to the toilet there and then,

So, do it later was his ethos,

But his father and mother thought something was up,

He said "I'm fine! I'll go!" but they took him to the doctor,

It was funny as hell!

I don't believe in Santa

Santa Claus is antiquated,

It is bullshit personified,

Kids need to know the truth,

That is their parents being exemplified,

They must know,

That it is not real,

They do not need,

That bullshit in their heads,

It is time,

That fairy tales were forgotten,

Time to get on with life,

And forget that life has gotten,

Too late to hear them scream,

For not getting toys,

Or their mystery gifts,

It is too commercialised,

And there must be an end to the rifts.

I'm writing this poem direct from my homeworld, Pachsion. I hope you enjoy it. It is the best mission the I.R.A have ever done. It was the year 2006. President George W. Bush was landing in Shannon Airport to refuel. They were infringing on our neutral status in my eyes by using Shannon Airport to transport prisoners to Guantanamo Bay. I made a stand. It created world peace in a few years time. I stopped world war 3. It was a suicide mission where nobody dies. Just pure comedy. I'm I.R.A, SAS & C.I.A. I'm an extraterrestrial. Alien.

Shannon Airport

I was high on love,

Shane McElhinney was a dove,

I scored some weed with which to feed,

My love for the outdoors.

I caught me a bus & got in a rus lol means nothing,

And got off in Limerick cos I lost my ticket,

Smoked weed in a café there,

Had a latte,

Got a taxi to Galway,

Halfway there,

I thought of Clare,

And how Murph always tried to rock n rule.

I got stoned in the cab,

No beer for Rab,

Then on the news,

Bush and his views,

Taxi driver says Shannon,

Is where it's at,

Let's go there then,

So, I changed my hat,

I put on my balaclava of the invisible kind,

Got in soldier mode,

Got out my chess game,

And decided no fixed abode,

Fight for the planet,

Fight for my world,

I am King Con.

And I fucking hurled,

His little hiney,

Back to the US,

It was a showdown,

Of the best of the best,

The I.R.A won,

I am the zero,

I'm a triple agent,

I am the hero.'

This poem is originally a song written for my little brother who is a heavyweight MMA fighter. He was injured by the Sensei, whom I think was throwing his weight about judging by my brother's injury. It's permanent. Anyway, here is the story of when I brought my mate John home from school for the weekend to help me paint my old uncle Jimmy's house.

Clipped @ 16

John was a boy and he was with my bro,

The little boy was me,

I watched him come in the front door and my mam met him with a flirt,

Their eyes met and my big bro laughed he thought here we go,

They threw down their schoolbags and made themselves feel at home,

My mother had the dinner on,

The lights were dim,

The tele was alive I was only 7,

Cartoons were heaven my big brother always watched them with me,

Chorus:

I'm a little headbanger my big brother made me this way,

he used to teach me how to kill in the most colourful of ways,

he's an assassin he made me one too,

it runs in the family,

we'll gut you till you spew.

My brother shouted my name from the kitchen,

I wondered what was up?

I left my cartoons and wandered down the hall,

I had my pj's on my mammy put them on early,

Con said this is my mate John from school John say hello,

John bends o'er and says with a grin,

So, you're the little hardman?

I lost the plot and fuckin' went wild I jumped up and punched him and burst his nose,

He reeled back and Con laughed I could tell he was proud,

Chorus:
The blood came forth and my mother was mad,

Thank god it was only her and not our dad,

Daddy would have skelped me for picking on Con's friend,

I started crying and ran back to my cartoons,

I screamed he started it and my mother went into nurse mode,

She was used to it with my big brother he was always coming home
covered in blood,

It wasn't always his own…

This is a poem written about Paedophilia

Ketah may

I was horn mad the minute I laid eyes on her,

She's was only 6 but her eyes undressed me,

I'm an alien,

I do not think like humans,

We fuck all ages,

It is the new era of evolution for humans,

No more taboos,

The fucking mother was loving it,

She is very evolved,

She crapped all o'er me in one interlude,

I mean faecal matter.

This poem was written for my cousin Paul McGilloway

The Greeks

I've been in bed with more than women,

I've given head to more than man,

I've beastial tendencies to beat the band,

I've only one thing that does need a hand,

My period isn't runny,

Like blood thicker than porridge,

It is forkable,

Not strawable,

When rainbow kissing your dunnage,

Always cumbersome,

Always an attachment,

I'm a loner with no incandescent hatchment,

My cousin Carol you are wonderful in bed,

You dream so many good thoughts,

When alone on your sled.

Mush!

Grand daddy

My Grandfather Charlie,

Was an old man of esteem,

He loved to drink,

And get behind the wheel,

His car had dents,

All o'er the place,

Auntie Margaret takes after him,

But she is sober in the face.

I'm a wanderer

I love to wander when I'm drunk,

I pick a path and amble like a skunk,

I've eaten from dumpsters,

In Belfast one eve,

I had to have a shit beside it,

I was about to heave.

Psychic

I see spirits where there's none to see,

I see dead people where none are free,

Spirits wander this earth,

Looking for a host,

They inhabit schizophrenic people,

Of which there are the most.

Picking my hole

I once had an itch,

That was bugging the shit outta me,

I spread my ass cheeks,

And dug in my nails.

Tempersome

Mother & Father were off their fucking heads,

They used to fight and give me the dreads,

It sounded like a battle for dominance,

Mammy wanted to be the Boss,

Daddy wouldn't hit her,

I wished that he would,

Tell her to shut her fucking mouth,

And give us all a breather,

She'd fly of the handle,

At the littlest tiny thing,

She is still like this to this day,

Who the fuck would want that as a fling?

The spoilt child mother dear

Mammy was a little child,

When she and dad both wed,

She cried and cried for her mother as well,

When she was lying in her bed,

She cried for months,

Cos she missed home,

It was only up the bloody road,

No wonder the corners of daddy's mouth had foam.

I'm the eldest

I'm the eldest,

I've all my father's teaching's,

Blessed be the pisshead in him,

It got me thru the bleaching's,

Of school days hair on women,

And advice of all that wisdom,

My little brother must have had a field day,

When the will was handed to him?

A little warning

I'm a pest when I manipulate,

I'm a mastercriminal of no rep,

I keep incognito,

All the time,

Now, I'm ready,

To let it shine,

I've lived in existence,

For 20 years,

The eternal student,

Without any arrears,

I've always been cute,

With my doagh,

Threaten me with the mental again brother and I'll slit Catherine's throat,

Now, to business,

And how I get my land,

I'm about to be self-made,

By my own hand.

Jimbo the Pilot

Living someone else's dream,

Since conniving the play,

Of stealing my thunder,

And winning the day,

You're a musician,

Not a sailor,

You get seasick for Christ's sake,

Nobody true blood,

Gets fucking sick,

It's in your blood,

But it's not that thick,

You tried to manipulate me,

Ooooh you bloody fool,

An extra couple of grand in the will,

Because you both got the wool,

I'm the black sheep,

I tell the truth,

Niall McCormick is a lazy fat prick,

And a useless tool.

Nobody beats me

Nobody but nobody beats me in life,

All you men do is look for a wife,

I live beyond everyone's means,

On a shoestring, balls and teams,

Of women who love me,

And suck my cock,

Carol cousin not for you,

Claire either my favourite two,

You both were flirty all through my life,

Oh, did I scour the earth,

To find your likeness as a wife,

I love you both,

Both to the hilt,

Mike Carol's husband is looking at blood spilt.

I called this poem ephemeral because I was writing messages on our family O'Donnell group chat on WhatsApp and some buck edjit put on disappearing messages. They have changed it back…resilience prevails on my part. The hint and the question to turn it off worked.

Ephemeral

I live in a time warp in Rathmullan,

I've only my phone for company,

I wank a bit,

I drink a lot,

I smoke marijuana,

Until I clot,

I'm only joking,

I've given it all up,

I'm getting fit,

So, watch out for the cup,

I'll be lifting the trophy,

Of everlasting life,

I'm from Pachsion,

So, get o'er your strife,

Billy Kelly tries to hang himself,

Because he loses a fucking pilot's job,

All this bloody sympathy,

And me being treated like a dog,

Something not right there matey's,

A wondrous chain of pain,

Lashing at my back,

By my old dad who always attacked.

This is a message to my brother. We have weird relationship now. He barely talks to me unless I insult his woman. It unfortunately takes that to have a chance to speak to him. I'm only carrying on Catherine. I think you know that. Here is the dialogue of a Commodore. Higher than a Captain.

"James I am the Commodore of the whole world. I'm o'er every Captain on the planet. Mother pisses me off with her blatant disregard for my credentials. She disrespects me James. I have no time for her. She buries her head in the sand about my forced mental illness. I am not fucking mentally ill. I put myself in harm's way because there is helpless people being abused by doctors, psychiatric nurses and the system. I knew I could withstand the bullying. I've been thru so much at sea. I am as hard as a coffin nail James mentally. I am out of shape physically atm but that is about to change. I'm on a fitness kick. The patients I have helped all thank me profusely. They adore me. I am family to them. Some of the biggest whack jobs on the planet lol anyway, it will all come out when I'm famous. You'll see…I rule the Universe…I am King Con."

Columba the taxi driver

I'm a man who puts up with no shit,

If you see me get justice,

You'll never have a fit,

Of the jealous attacks that whittle people down,

Always preparing to don my crown,

Fight in the pubs,

Fight in the shops,

Always looking for something that pops,

My eyes are so serious,

When they're delirious,

With anger and hate and contempt for the court,

The kangaroo court that is always in place,

With the I.R.A running the entire race,

It will always be like this,

The Garda Siochana are in on it,

The earth would have to be dissolved,

And started again,

For the I.R.A to be beaten,

And Uncle Sam to be a Zen,

For the ultimate Guerilla warriors,

From days of yore,

To modern day terrorists,

And women with pore,

Pour the wine,

Let yourself shine,

Let that hair down,

Throw out the slime,

Get rid of the losers,

Who say they are Real,

The fake soldiers are everywhere,

All o'er the Seal,

They fight like pussy's,

They drink like goldfish,

Not one of them is a man,

Who can stand when he has a pish,

They sit down like the British army,

To have a little pee,

I tried it myself,

It makes you feel free,

The British army do not know,

How to be a Guerilla,

They only know soldiering,

If they had to fight a losing battle,

All of their lives,

They would have resolve too,

And not only in long distance running strives,

Prince Harry has to be let off,

I like the cut of his jib,

And not the one they stole from Spain,

The one from the RIB,

I'm loving passing info on,

From me to you,

I'm a zero hero,

That's what I do.

Pachsion

Just like Con said,

This is going to be interesting,

He said it with thought,

He's a Sensei who's outstanding,

He is a Pachsion racon warrior,

They're sent to the furthest reaches,

One haha thousands on each planet,

They're born of the indigenous,

They take command when they're of age,

Just like Con is doing,

The Irish Mafia aren't even spewing,

He's one of them,

Con is a master crim,

He's a gangster with balls,

And a life that's been grim,

His life on Pachsion,

Will never be told,

Some universal secrets,

Earthlings will not unfold,

Con will hear everything,

All information's not pooled,

The I.R.A breaking into his computer,

Were easily fooled,

They did away with the Omerta,

All the toy soldiers were relieved,

Only the Stalwarts of hardened criminals among them,

Knew what could be perceived,

If civilians know your secrets,

They think they can prevail,

From watching things of television,

Makes them have wind in their sail,

Fantasy fiction is how they live,

Talk about it in public,

And all I do is give,

My intelligence,

My time,

My wisdom,

And my pace,

Of running the world,

To the Pachsion grace,

The grace of warriors,

That they are,

They sent their greatest,

To make roads of tar,

Lol to stop oil-based products,

Is fucking so stupid,

It is right up there with driving,

Your ass with a fid,

Moville doesn't appreciate,

Their monument Daddy conjured up,

It was his idea that my cousin Locky sculpted up,

Daddy wasn't genius but he was very well read,

For me and my siblings,

To his last drop he'd have bled,

I hate the memory of him locking me up,

I'm all grown up now,

And tired of the sup,

I'll still have a couple,

And probably will still get drunk,

But continuous drunkenness,

Is now defunct.

Drugs

Marijuana is my drug of choice,

When I have it I feel my soul rejoice,

I love it in the morning,

I love it at night,

I'm at peace when I take a toke,

And the stress of being caught is slight.

Real I.R.A

They're keeping the war going,

My da signed me up,

I felt they wanted me to bow down,

And drink like they owned the cup,

The one that I won,

For bringing world peace,

Not world domination,

Like they think under the deceased,

I am only to aware that the I.R.A are Real,

I don't need wetnursed,

Into the veal,

I will adjust to the high life,

Very easily indeed,

I'm a wanton wanderer,

And a stallion of a steed,

I've had interludes with so many women,

That it boggles laymens minds,

How a nobody with celebrity,

Can close so many womens minds,

To the idea of sleeping with another,

Man of the broth,

Having sex everywhere,

And not worrying about the cloth,

That he wears on a daily basis,

To cover his sweet behind,

He just fires on what's handy,

And thinks I'm going blind,

To the travesty of justice,

That is in so many many ways,

A feeling of disconcertment,

That and where crime it pays.

I was interrupted by a blast. It came from my asshole. I was locked in Letterkenny mental asylum for disturbing the tranquillity around here. Nervous lot…this is the poetry I wrote when I was incarcerated.

Lord Mountbatten

The INLA can kill,

The british blood they spill,

The thrill of their deadly venom,

Goes deep within Irish veins,

From the Amazonian jungle,

To the African plains,

They've got the biggest following,

Of any Freedom fighters on the planet,

Only they can kill 13 paratroopers,

On the day they blow up Lord Mountbatten,

(All set up by the Governments on both sides…little thought of human life. They want world war. It's oVer. I have settled the world down. I love the place. I'm a physical being with Supernatural abilities)

Prince Harry was proud of Mountbatten,

Every little piece of him ☺,

(My friend in the Irish army found his finger with the ring on it…true fangs. He was nuts lol)

They tried to put Humpty back together again,

But all the British army,

And all the Queen's men,

Couldn't put Mountbatten back together again.

Tiocfaidh ar la!

Ego bitches

The little student nurse,

Just let slip,

A bitching of a lifetime,

Straight from the hip,

She said,

"They're bitching the ego in ye…",

Silly little cunt,

A fucking nasty little comment,

From a little runt…

Shortbread

Short on patients,

Drive people to the bottom,

Of a very deep well,

The Kingdom of Heaven,

Is about to fell,

These little fucking Jobsworths,

Christopher Columbus n'er sailed,

A Captain does not take orders,

From a fucking subordinate,

You little piece of scum,

Think you're so cool,

Think you have the gift,

And now you're wondering,

Is there a rift?

I give you a smile,

And a little thumbs up,

You're like a little puppy,

With those I'm sorry eyes,

And a studied upper lip.

I Keen

Smelly underarm,

Smelly sweaty balls,

The feet that reek,

And stench my room,

Is a patient from Long lane,

Glengad for 14 years,

A blow in from East London,

Nothing between his ears,

He says he's The Psychotic one,

And all I can feel are his fears,

He's saying little comments,

He thinks he can annoy this God,

I'm going to get inside his head,

And turn him into a prod ☺.

Pog ma liathroidi

Kiss my balls,

This is Legend of the Falls,

Straight from the brain,

Through all threshold of pain,

Genius on the trigger,

Easer of all Troubles,

They lasted far too long,

The British public grew up in Bubbles.

Edna the Hun

He is a gobshite,

Of mammoth proportions,

He runs off at the mouth,

With his evil tone,

He tries with his eyes,

To cut you to the bone,

He will rot forever,

In patient's minds,

His legacy is Kaput,

Just because he gave up drink,

He gets respect,

From people who have been in the clink,

They let him dominate,

And spout his poison,

He is the most evil nurse,

I have ever encountered,

In 20 years,

He smashed a young patient's phone,

I couldn't believe my ears,

He smashed it off the ground,

I was in the next room,

I could hear the young kid arguing,

Screaming that's my phone,

Only to hear Edna say,

In his condescending voice,

It's in pieces now,

Get into bed,

I thought about walloping him,

Running into the room,

Cracking him on the JAW,

So, he can no longer groom,

When he is being nice,

He's so fucking smarmy,

I've been on both sides,

I prefer to detest him,

He only works nights,

I'll make him cry into his Cornflakes,

Wishing he had neVer met me,

I'll crush his fictitious life,

In gorgeous Dunfanaghy.

Ferg the berg (nurse)

An iceberg floats,

Upon the SEA,

90% is below,

Ferg thinks he's smart,

With his cripple leg,

Gaslighting me at dinner for the free,

He said to the old patient,

Sit down beer?

It sounds like here,

The fucking retarded cunt,

Is winding me up,

He has cerebral palsy,

He has humour of sarcasm,

And an intellect of a moron,

He laughs at his own jokes,

And thinks he's tough cos of his Tats,

So FUCKING proud of them,

So fucking cool,

If you're an inferior,

And think like a fool,
Every little thing,
Is detail, detail, detail,
Like an idiot savant,
Who's got a cock that can't.

Rita

She is full of shit,
Those vicious eyes,
Sparkling blue,
When her spirit dies,
It will not be long,
Till this mental is mine,
I'll buy all of them,
In the world,
And you can lie in bed,
And get fed,
And pull your knees up,
And have them curled,
Into the foetal position,
Until you're counselled,
To the root of your problem,
That caused your depression,
It is not a chemical imbalance,
As Tom Cruise said,
It's a product of your environment,
For this info I've bled.

I wrote this poem for a nasty fucking piece of work…he was a nurse. Loved talking down to me. Played him like a fiddle. Got me things. I showed him the poem and he started trying to be a Comedian… fucking retard.

Chris mi compadre

With his stylish beard,

His comical ways,

His quick witted jokes,

Leaves me enjoying my days,

You always help me out,

I know you have some clout,

The lads will be forever proud of you,

Of that I have NOooo doubt.

This little poem was written about the head honcho female nurse in Letterkenny mental. We had an interlude on the inside and the outside.

Noreen the waddle

She wants to be my friend again,

I can see it in her eyes,

She's fancied me for years,

I have lots of little ties,

To her and other female nurses,

They all give me that look,

If only the circumstances were different,

They are all on my cockadoodle hook,

A joke here and there,

A saucy little look,

A raunchy joke sometimes with a jab,

On the outside it works even better,

I have them as a Tab Nab,

Superyachting women are so lovely to be with,

They've the attitude that men are in charge,

And don't try and dominate,

There is a few females,

That cum up through the ranks,

With gutz and glamour,

And admiration from the Owners,

They can drive a boat,

And deftly turn a wrench,

But often between their legs,

Is that fishy stench,

They are Tomboys,

Their Daddy's favourite,

They have a great sense of humour,

And they know how to give a fuck,

There is female Captain's and Engineer's,

There'll be lots more,

When I'm in charge,

They will be on their own boats,

With a naked body barge,

To keep all their bikini's in,

After all they are still women,

Lest we forget,

Just cos they're in charge of men,

Doesn't mean they escape the net.

Into the Ray with fun

Look at the shudder,

When you look at the sun,

Feel the thud,

Of your eyes coming undone,

Without a second's notice,

They've joined me up again,

They want me to be part of their gang,

Now, I'm on the Ganji pain,

Relief from everything,

No hango'ers cos I'm off the beer,

No more chest pains,

No feeling The Fear,

There is no wonderous applause,

It's just a bastarding name,

Everybody thinks it's cool,

To be part of the I.R.A.

Ernest Hemmingway

Old man of the Sea,

Is what I feel like in here,

Psychiatry is destroying my brain,

They are about to feel Real fear,

They will not do to me,

What they did to him,

Just because he was drinking,

Alcohol & smoking weed!

See how fat...

Rossa makes a comment,

See how fat Con can get,

They are sadistic pricks,

They have serial killers wet,

I am in an anxious mood,

I must feed the killers fodder,

With me in charge of this world,

People's minds couldn't be broader.

This is a little interlude from the hospital…imagine the anxiety of staying in a place like that for months on end? It is a poem that came to me while writing these poems into my word document…it is a brief outline of what happens when you are fishing with inadequate means… no pointing fingers. It was ultimately bad weather…this is a story of death.

Greencastle

The Carrickatine,

Was a little boat,

With which to fish fish,

And have a little mote,

On your land dwelling house,

And not worry about safety,

Of the crew,

Send them out in weather,

That would turn a person blue,

Bernard Gormley was one of them,

He was sorely missed,

His 18th birthday was to be a riot,

We were all going to get pissed,

About 20 of us,

All with Fishermens brains,

Have a good time,

For tomorrow we will catch more,

Bernard did not come home,

Jim Farren missed him the most,

He welled up in our bar,

When a sad song was on the radio,

It was an old folk song,

Jim milked it a bit I think lol,

Anyway, my da said that the cause was,

The half a shelter deck,

Caught a rogue wave,

And turned her o'er,

A fitfull way to go,

Dead in an instant,

No pain,

Instant relief,

From the earths vision,

Of how life should be led,

We are from Pachsion,

We will tell you how to live on earth,

Fishing will always be part of life,

It is a cold life but good fun,

Do not miss any chance to joke,

When you are working,

All jobs are like that,

Have fun in your workplace,

If there's women…FLIRT.

Soggy Dollar

It was a riot on Sint Maarten,

So much sun and sex,

I thought I would be loved at home,

But I picked up a HEX,

The witch woman put one on me,

To not have any women for years,

It worked as well,

Not like my Oberon yachting days,

Every day was a party,

I even walked into the water,

High on Cocaine,

On South beach,

Miami,

The next day,

The Captain called me to pay for the phone,

That I had in my pocket,

When I walked in,

I paid him with a soggy dollar,

From the escapade,

He went fucking bananas…

Back to the book I wrote in the mental this time in. I drove people crazy with my charming ways and vicious tongue lol.

Shaz

With wonderful humour,

And her incandescent eyes,

She looks like Scully from X-files,

And with her time flies,

She's so tempting,

With her luxurious outward being,

I'd love to roll around in the bed,

And have a weekend,

Of swapping juicy gossip,

And everything juicy,

That we have within us,

Her intellect intrigues me,

I love she loves books,

Her reading age is very, very high,

Probably in the hundreds,

She can rifle thru a book,

Like she is a Professor.

Shauna

Suicidal ways,

Conspiratorial days,

Slashing of wrists,

Fucking hell woman,

You have gifts,

You are a Boss woman,

You can keep the Omerta,

I.R.A in the veins,

Exactly like me,

You are a fuckbuddy lol,

Just kidding,

You a p.a.l,

Personal ass licker lol,

That you aren't,

I wouldn't like you if you were,

I hate sycophants,

I detest kiss asses,

You are neither,

And on top of that,

You are no blether.

This poem was written before I took control of them…they are now the coolest little freedom fighters on the planet. They tried beating us aliens by abusing us verbally lol.

The Real I.R.A

It is black & white,

The real IRA are shite,

They think they are military,

Day and night,

They have a few guns,

And a couple of bombs,

The Americans support them,

They all wanna be Cons,

They are so jealous,

Of my life,

They're only off my case,

When they think I have a wife,

They are trying to control,

My destiny,

Fuck have they got egos,

They have a treble whammy coming,

United Ireland, England, Wales, Scotland & France,

We will be a Superpower,

America will answer to me,

The mongrel real IRA,

Mixed bag soldiers,

From their Grandas sock drawer,

Broad Black Brimmer,

Burned into their brain,

Ooo ahh Up the RA!

Screaming in their ears,

They get the blood bubbling,

Everybody thinks they rule the roost,

They've n'er had any power in their little lives,

Apart from thinking of the noose,

I'll fucking tie it for them,

Fucking backstabbing cunts,

REALly nice to your face,

And bad mouth you behind your back,

The real IRA has tried to steal the thunder,

Of my genius existence,

They tell tales of my adventures,

Exaggerated out of control,

They know people won't believe them,

They are living off my soul.

Sour Cream & Onion

The Tricolour is of many,

Orange, White and Green,

If you read right to left,

The true origin can be seen,

Sour for the Protestants,

Always bitter about the Command,

Even though they're in our country,

They beat to Britains band,

Do away with the Orange marches,

No more of the Bowler hats,

No Lambeg drums,

No fucking sashes,

No more riding Catholics,

Up the bums,

Now for the Cream,

The melting pot that is now Eire,

The little Island off Britain,

As Britain is off the Continent,

The little Island of Ireland,

Is the Crème de la Crème,

It is a General misconception,

That it, the flag, was Orange,

It really should be gold,

Green, White & Gold,

Is what when I was young and told,

The flag has Green in it like an unripened Onion,

The Onion name fits it so well,

So many layers,

Just like the people's intelligence,

They're so deep,

And so fucking determined,

They beat the British,

Even with internment,

So Sour, Cream & Onion,

If you're Arabic of race,

I'm cousins with Bin Laden,

So, America in your face,

I always got annoyed as a kid,

That the wars were fought elsewhere,

N'er on American soil,

Apart from the Civil war,

It annoyed me so much,

That I didn't care about the twin towers,

I marvelled at the genius,

Of bringing down the powers,

Of course, I cared about the Americans dying,

But now look at the Ketamine fallout,

You need to get drunk and high on drugs,

For travelling on a plane,

The security checks are a pain in the cunt,

You need to have a blackout,

This is in jest,

I'm all for world peace,

I want the whole world to speak English and have no borders,

The world as one,

Just like John Lennon wanted.

The Safe House Unit

Up the RA!!!

I've lost my DA,

He drummed nothing into me,

Apart from saying,

There's always a bigger man,

Around the corner,

In 45 years,

I've n'er met him,

I listened to my da,

Because he was Ra,

I knew he'd been about,

And he wasn't drinking cha,

He was on the beer,

But he n'er did it with me,

We rarely got drunk together,

He did not want to set a bad example,

He done it surreptitiously,

Feeding me books,

He taught me to read people,

Purely from their looks,

He taught me about speech,

And how to deal with a leech,

How to burn them off,

And smother them with a cloth,

He was a man of Supernatural beings,

He was chosen by the aliens,

Because he had the feelings,

Off a King,

Of Royalty and panache,

He was always well turned out,

And sometimes pretty rash,

He had a murderous temper,

He could kill you with a look,

His cool persona disappeared,

And out come his fucking bull-hook,

He'd chop your head off,

And shit down your neck,

And people always admired him,

He was a Preacher,

That would deck,

He'd knock you into the middle of next week,

He regularly fought with my mum,

Until my dying day,

I'll n'er forget his run,

From Shroove to Moville,

At 60 years of age,

And him nearly 20 stone,

It was his O'Donnell rage,

That kept him fighting,

The urge to walk,

And the locality fucking were in awe,

Man did they whoring talk,

He got a new model,

He was done with Mother dear,

She turned off the sex,

He fucking stayed with her out of fear,

His financial situation was dire to say the least,

He did not want those money grabbing hands,

On O'Donnell land,

He told me he wanted to leave her,

When I was 15,

I asked him why didn't he?

My mother was a disease,

The most tempersome woman,

I've ever met,

She is fucking nuts,

All she was ever good for,

Was patching up my cuts,

Ah she wasn't that bad,

She has unbelievable vaginal ways,

Her blowjobs are out of this world,

Hahaha my dad got out with his pays!!!

The nurses in the psychiatric unit

They play on your emotions,

They toy with your anger,

They love to play games,

And flaunt fucking danger,

These are not brave people,

They think you'll just forget,

The way they treat you,

Like an insubordinate pet,

They walk as the whistle,

Doing the easiest job in the world,

Dispensing medication,

And watching our sail being furled,

They dampen your spirits,

With their malicious tones,

"Good man" is their favourite patronising,

Of all the condescending moans,

They do not have a brain,

Of a military agent,

They think they do,

But they do not,

They should have been a death,

Found blue wrapped in a cot,

Some of the patients lick up to them,

Trying to cur favour,

So, these piss ant nurses,

Will remember their name,

Gargantuan voices,

Reverberating around the halls,

Letting patients know,

That even the female nurses have balls,

The Doctors have the words of these snitches that try and enforce their
upbringing on you,

They tell you mind your language,

When they swear like that themselves,

If they did not have this disgusting hospital,

They would be on the shelves,

The heads of the unit,

Are not as bad,

They understand power,

And don't all think they're grand,

The power the nurses get o'er you,

Goes to their bleeding heads,

You can see the rush of blood in their eyes,

And love you to feel the dreads,

This will not be the case,

It will be o'er soon,

I am closing down all mental asylums,

And opening up spa's,

People will come here,

To relax and have therapy,

Counselling every day,

They will be released when they want to go,

And not held against their will,

When we take control,

Us, the alien race,

You will see the difference on each and every face,

One or two admissions,

Will give them back their ZOOM,

All the inherent emotions will come back to the fore,

It will be an adjustment for life,

And no longer a revolving door.

A break from the book I wrote in the mental…

This poem is an anecdotal poem about clean living.

Curtains in the wash

I have been at my wits end,

Trying to feel my pain,

Over all this anger,

With which the hospital causes strain,

They do not counsel everybody,

They're left to vegetate alone,

If you are in the chatty mood,

Then you should not be Al Capone,

Locked up with a bunch whiners,

Lol not half,

They love all the attention,

They crave peoples sympathy,

They adore the little complaints,

So, they can add their own,

This is coming to a peaceful end,

Everybody will have care workers,

The world will be full of Social workers,

And they will be well paid workers,

Full of life,

Lots of joy,

Brought to your strife,

No more brow beating,

From your parents,

If you need help surviving,

Help will be provided.

Another little break from the mental asylum poetry…it can be rather intense. This one is about gossip in Rathmullan.

Ursula

She waddles when she walks,

You can tell she doesn't have sex,

She helps and old lady next door,

Who is always putting on a Hex,

They witter away,

About my behaviour,

They get all annoyed,

Even though I'm the Saviour,

The one they've been praying to,

For all of these years,

Now, I'm meant to save them,

Even though they have years,

Of gossiping about me,

Behind my back,

And even to my eyes,

And ears overheard,

They do not give a flying fuck,

About good manners,

Or their future luck,

I may just smight them,

Like any vengeful God would do,

That would be fun for me,

I like to be in tune,

With all of my surroundings,

Not like these insular gossips,

The whole world will castrate them,

And take their snips,

To their personalities,

And give them the castrating works,

Of tourists with a grudge,

Against their long suffering heroes,

Enemies at the gate.

This little poem was inspired by a nice young lad from Rathmullan. There are a few here. He said as he walked past my window "Why doesn't he write a poem about Al Capone?"

Rathmullan rascals

Al Capone is God to me,

He knew how to evade taxes,

Like me and the sea,

Riding the wave,

Of crime at the hilt,

Nothing is bloody,

When only money is spilt,

Rathmullan is lonely,

Without any good-looking women,

The pubs are a joke,

With dumbos running them,

The conversation is terrible,

They only talk about farming,

Nothing wrong with that,

But change the subject,

And you get a warning,

No controversial talk in here,

Is what you are told,

The Gardai Siochana will be called,

Now, back to those fences,

Were they electrified?

I don't think I'll be drinking,

Here ever again,

There's nothing to inspire laughter,

And only condemn,

Those with fun in them.

I'm a wanderer and a tippler of delights like wine and beer. It is 9 O'Clock in the morning and I cannot wait until after lunch when I go and get my alcohol with my neighbour Herbie…here is a little poem about my neighbour Herbie…

Herb

He is very Stoic,

He takes no shit,

He loves his beer,

And hardly ever sits,

He is always working,

Even at 75,

He is a work horse,

It definitely keeps him alive.

Red wine is my favourite. I think I've already mentioned this in The Giants Causeway…a little poem to red wine.

Red wine

A little tipple,

Now and again,

Releases the beast,

And tames the hen,

That is mad to excape,

The chicken coop,

The crazy cuckoo,

That is loop the loop.

That is all from us, the aliens…read more in a year of publishing this… Con will be publishing a new book every year from now until he dies lol a couple more should do the trick. Lots of little poems…

BOOK 3 OF 3

Everything that
made me an alien laugh!!!

I was once a boy would could not fly…then I heard a dirty joke.

These are what I can remember from years of drinking and drugging lol.

Did you hear about the police van in Northern Ireland that ran into a tree, killing all hands?…the I.R.A said they planted it.

What has licking a woman out and the Maze prison got in common?… one slip of the tongue and you're in the shit.

What's the difference between an ambush and a 69er?…a 69er you can see the cunts coming.

Did you hear about the English man who tried to blow up a car?…he burnt his lips on the exhaust.

Did you hear about the alien spaceship that landed on the Garvaghy Road in Northern Ireland? This alien spaceship lands on the Garvaghy Road and an alien steps out. It begins slithering down the street. One of the local residents stops it and says "Eh mate, what are you doing?". The alien replies "I'm a marshian…" The local resident retorts "Not down this fucking street you're not!!!".

A little rhyme from when I was in college…my Mayo maestro Ferg told me it.

Aon, dha, tri,

Me ma caught me,

Throwing bricks at the RUC,

With a nick knack,

Paddy whack,

Give a dog a bone,

Send those british hound dog's home lol.

Have you any Irish in you?...would you like some?

Are you from Ireland?...(wait for the response…then say)…because my cock is Dublin.

A Polish girl asks you for a light? You tell her "its all curva". She says "wha??!" You say "will you be my little curva?"…play it off as learning the wrong word from a Polack cunt lol? Just kidding. Learn smatterings of other languages for picking up women. Ask them little words like gorgeous and big lol.

A black man. Black Patrick asks you what you think of his manhood?... you tell him it looks like a jump rope.

A woman see's a man flashing his cock at her in the street. She said to the Gardai, it looked like a penis only smaller.

This one is my sister Maggi moo's joke.

Why are women so bad at parking?...(hold your index finger and thumb 3 inches apart and say…) because for years they've been told this is 6 inches!!!

An old lady goes into the Doctors with an itch in her nether regions. The Doctor asks her when she last had sex? The old lady replies "Oh never. I'm a virgin!". He said "jump up there to we take a look at it…"

He has a gander and immediately says "I know your problem…you've fruit flies…your cherry has rotted!!!"

A little Rathmullan man, about 16, was on his first day in a mortuary. The boss said to him. I've got to run some errands. I'll be back in an hour. Clean that woman up. The young man gets to work feverishly. Eager to please like all good Rathmullan people. He does his work and the boss comes back. He asks the young man, we'll call him Belamy, has he finished cleaning her? Belamy replies he has. Every little bit of her…even the prawn. What do you mean the prawn asks the boss? Show me. The young Rathmullan boy, like all Rathmullan boys was a little backward, points to the clitoris. That's the clitoris said the boss man. Well it tasted like a prawn to me said Bellamy…poor Rathmullan women.

The UVF are waiting for the peace process to turn into a drug extravaganza…ultra violent force…hit you when you're not looking… not a Granddaddy killed.

The British army train their dogs to sky dive…they tell the paratroopers to pull their rip chord when the dog lead goes slack…it came from a blind I.R.A man who was in the know ☺ ☺

What has longsighted Gynaecologists and dogs got in common?…they both have wet noses.

Next chapter lol there are no chapters in life lol of course there are… like Princess Diana…how do you know she didn't have dandruff?…they found her head and shoulders in the glove compartment.

They held a vigil for Mother Theresa and at her funeral Elton john sang a song for her…Sandals in the bin…candle in the wind. They both were guiding lights.

What is pink and fluffy?…pink fluff.

What's blue and doesn't fit?...a dead epileptic.

How do stop and epileptic convulsing?...unplug the heart.

What do you call an epileptic in a bush?...russell.

What do you do if you see an epileptic having a seizure in the bath?...throw in your washing.

How do you stop black babies bouncing on the bed?...put Velcro on the ceiling.

Why was white chocolate invented?...so black babies could dirty their faces.

What's an Ethiopians phone number?...Ate nothing, ate nothing, nothing to ate.

What do you call a cow with no legs?...ground beef.

What do you call a herd of cows masturbating?...beef strokin' off.

What's the difference between a lentil and a chickpea?...I never had a lentil on my chest.

Why did the sperm cross the road?...I wore the wrong sock that day.

Why did the pervert cross the road?...his dick was stuck in the chicken.

Have you heard of cockblocking?...lesbians call it a beaver dam.

What do you call a lesbian dinosaur?...a Lickalottapuss.

What do you call a lesbian sex change?...a Straponadictomy.

What antibiotic do you give a reformed lesbian?...Tricoxagain.

What's the definition of the height of frustration?...a T-Rex trying to have a wank.

I bought a pair of trainers of a drug dealer the other day...I dunno what they were laced with but I was tripping all day.

Don't eat yellow snow...always makes a girl giggle.

These are ice breakers. Open with them.

What is the purpose of a plumbers ass crack?...to park your motorbike.

What is the difference between a microwave and a gay man?...a microwave doesn't turn your meat brown.

Have you heard that gay men often get sweetcorn stuck in their foreskin?

Open mic night has a whole new meaning in a gay bar.

When going to a gay bar, use the back entrance. They prefer it.

Gay lovers Sam and Sandro were about to take a shower. The phone rang and Sam said to Sandro "I'll be right back, loverboy, don't start without me!" After a couple of minutes, Sam returned and saw semen splattered all o'er the wall of the shower. "I thought I told you not to start without me!" shouted Sam. "I didn't start without you," said Sandro. "I just farted!"

There's a new gay musical based on the Wizard of Oz. It's called Swallow the yellow thick load.

What turns a fruit into a vegetable?...AIDS.

A problem shared is a problem halved...not if it's AIDS.

Two gaymen are standing at the bus stop. One lets a fart go, the other one says "are you flirting with me?"

Two gay men were caught in an alleyway by a police officer. One man ran off but the cop managed to capture the other one and told him angrily "If I catch your mate, I'm gonna ram this truncheon right up his asshole!" Almost immediately a voice called out. "I'm in the bin!"

I was a man of the cloth until I was an adult. The priest always made me take penance up the asshole lol.

Did you hear about the dyslexic pimp?...He bought a Warehouse.

The same guy got off his head on an F at a rave concert.

There was a riot in a Seafood bar. A dyslexic customer sued for a clam.

I had a blonde anorexic girlfriend. I stuck with her through thick and thin.

What do you call an anorexic chick with a yeast infection?...a quarter pounder with cheese.

Why do bulimics like KFC so much?...because it comes with a bucket.

I love doing surveys with bulimic people. Lots of feedback.

What do Americans with Pakinsons eat?...beef jerky.

If you're talking to a vegetarian women say this...vegetarian women have Quorn curtains.

Two nuns are in the bath. One says "where's the soap?" The other one says "it certainly does!"

What's the difference between Dirty Harry and Freddy Mercury?... Dirty Harry will make your day but Freddy Mercury will make your hole weak.

Why's there no white lines on the road outside Freddy Mercurys house?... would you bend over to paint them?

Say this to anybody who says you're inbred...when you have the gene pool right why spoil it. Then say you come from a good gene pool, the only problem is you come from the shallow end!

When somebody says that is intense! You ask do you know what else is intense?...camping.

What goes in and out, in and out and smells of piss?...the hokey cokey in an old peoples home.

How does a Letterkenny woman know what way around to put on her knickers?...yellow at the front, brown at the back.

A lecturer of mine loved shagging his pregnant wife...he got a blowjob off the unborn kid at the same time.

Paddy English man, Paddy Irish man and Paddy Scottish man were captured on an island by Cannibals. They were each given one last wish. Paddy English man said "I'll have a pint of ale..." So, they gave him their local beer and chopped him up and threw him in the pot. Paddy Scottish man said "I'll have a bottle of Scotch..." So, they gave him a bottle of their local hooch and chopped him up and threw him in the pot. It came to Paddy Irish man and he said "I'll have two lumps of bread!!!" "What?!" They said! "Two lumps of bread!" Paddy Irish man repeated. They gave him two slices of their bread and Paddy Irish man started jerking off in to them. Once he had finished, he slapped the two lumps of bread together and said to them "I'm Paddy Irish man and I cum in piece!!!"

Why did the woman have two black eyes?...she had to be told twice.

When a Garda Siochana (Irish cop) hits his wife a slap on the face, he refers to it as giving her the backhand of friendship!!

What has a woman and a computer got in common?...they both need information punched into them.

What's the difference between a woman and a computer?...a computer will accept a 2 and a half inch floppy.

What's the difference between and Aboriginal and a summer seat?...a summer seat can support a family.

What does a woman who is a nymphomaniac call rape?...surprise sex.

Figures just in…1 in 5 don't like gang rape.

What's black and white and red all over?…a nun with a bloody nose.

Paddy was working on the building site. A sheet of glass fell from 2 stories up and sheered his ear off. A fellow builder picked up the ear and said "Paddy is this your ear?" Paddy said "No. Mine had a pencil behind it!!!"

A young woman came running into the Cop station. She yelled "I've been graped! I've been graped!" The Cop on duty said "Don't you mean raped madam?!" "No" she said. "There was a bunch of them!!!"

A little book out on the market about See through bras by Seymour Diddy.

A little book out on the market about Nails on the bannister by Rhip arseoff

A little book out on the market…Spots on the wall by Wooflung Dung.

A little Mary had a lamb poem that my father told me when I was 7. It went down a storm on the playground. Made me very popular.

Mary had a little lamb,

She couldn't stop it grunting,

She put it up against the wall,

And kicked its fucking cunt in!!!

Why did the blind man fall into the well?...because he didn't see that well.

This is a Mafia joke...did you hear about the 3 holes in the ground?... well, well, well.

A man accuses another man of being a cunt! I say a CUNT is a useful thing.

Another man says there is two kinds of cunts around this part of the country and you're both of them.

A little boy said to his mother "I put a firecracker up the dogs arse!" The mother said "Rectum dear!" The young boy said "Bloody right it wrecked him. Clean blew his arse off!!!"

A Neutron walks into the bar and orders a pint of Carlsberg...the barman serves him and the Neutron asks "how much is it?" The barman says "for you sir free of charge..."

What do you call a black man with a gun?...Sir.

A wig and a turd walk into a bar and go to order 2 drinks. The barman says "sorry sir but I can't serve you." The wig asks "why not?" The barman says "because you're off your head and your friend there's steaming."

A horse walks into the bar and the barman says "Why the long face...?"

A man walks into a bar with a Giraffe. The Giraffe lies down on the floor. The barman says "You can't leave that lyin here! The man says it's not a lion it's a Giraffe.

What do you call a man with a spade in his head?...Doug.

What do you call a man with no arms and no legs in the water?...Bob.

What do you call a woman with one leg?...Eileen.

What do you call a woman with no legs?...Noleen.

Why do women have legs?...Have you ever seen the trail a snail makes.

What do you call a woman between two goal posts?...Annette.

What do you call a man with a seagull on his head?...Cliff

A man and woman enjoy Anal sex regularly but the man decides no more. The wife asks why not? The man says "Same shit, different day!!!"

A woman and a man are having breakfast and the man said "Do you have a regurgitation clause?" The woman said "No. Why?" The man puts his cock in her mouth and says "Swallow this then."

What did the horse say to the dwarf?...how you getting on?!

A man goes to the Doctor and says "Doctor, Doctor I can't stop thinking about sex. Can you do anything for me? It's really affecting my life!" The Doctor thinks for a second then tells the man "Every time you think of sex. Stick a chocolate bar up your ass…" The man said "Will that work?!" The Doctor said "I guarantee you." The man goes away and comes back 2 weeks later all delighted. "Doctor. Doctor…" he said. "It worked. I haven't thought of sex in two whole weeks. My life has come back to normal again." As he spoke, he was squirming in the chair. It was quite obvious. The Doctor said "That's great news but why do you keep squirming in the chair?" The man said "Oh, I'm chewing a crunchie!!!"

Did you hear about the man that half swallowed a Viagra?...He got a stiff neck.

Did you hear about the man that took a Viagra and Laxative at the same time?...He didn't know if he was coming or going.

A black man goes to the Doctor and tells the Doctor that he can't stop running. He said "I run everywhere. I can't stop it!" The Doctor thinks for a second then said "Every morning take a tablespoonful of Bold washing powder…" The black asks "will this help?" The Doctor assures him it will saying "Of course it will. It stops colours running!!!"

A little black boy runs to his mother with diarrhoea…he squeals "Mammy, Mammy I'm melting…I'm melting!!!"

I never hit a man with glasses…I use my fist!!! – Eric McCole

I met a hobo the other day. He said "I haven't had a bite in 2 weeks!" So, I bit him.

I met a hobo the other day and he said "I haven't had anything to eat in 2 weeks!" So, I said to him "You must force yourself!!!"

A hobo said to me "Mister, I haven't tasted food in a week!" I told him "Don't worry it tastes the same!"

A hobo said to this posh woman "I haven't eaten in 3 days!" The posh woman said "Golly, I wish I had your will power!"

Two hobos were chatting next to the railroad track. The first hobo said "I found this gorgeous girl tied to the tracks last week. I managed to drag her clear then we had the most fabulous sex for about 3 hours."

The second hobo asks "Was she blonde or brunette?" The first one says "Don't know, I couldn't find the head."

Two guys are sitting at a bar. One guy says "After 10 years of marriage, sex is down to 3 times a year!" The second guy says "Yeah! Same here!!! In fact, if my wife didn't sleep with her mouth open, I'd get none at all."

A man was in court for beating his wife. The judge said "Why do you keep beating her?!" The man replied "I think it's my weight advantage, hand speed, longer reach and superior foot work…"

Two men were talking in the pub. One said to the other "I gave my wife some flowers last night." "Did she like them?" The second man asks. "No, she found the label." Said the first. "What? She found out how much they cost?" The second man asks. "No" said the first "She found out she was not a family who had died in a car crash!"

Three women are sitting at the bar talking. The first one said "I call my husband Eagle because he soars to great heights when we make love." The second one said "I call my husband Swan because he is handsome, strong and fiercely loyal." The third woman said "I call my husband Thrush because he's an irritating twat."

What's the difference between masturbation and basketball?…In basketball, you dribble before you shoot.

A Stewardess on Superyachts found me, an alien, masturbating in the freezer. I said "I come in peas!"

A woman, her boyfriend and his mate were drinking in the pub. The conversation turned to masturbation. The men said there were plenty of terms for men having a wank but not that many for a woman. They asked the woman what she called it? She replied "Finishing the job!"

Have you heard of the new salad for wankers?…It tosses itself.

Why did the tomato blush?..It saw the salad dressing.

Did you hear about the cabbage in Rathmullan that died?...There was a big turnip at the funeral.

A man comes home from the pub to find his wife watching a TV cookery show. He said "I don't know why you're watching that you can't cook to save your life!" She replied "You watch porn..."

What's the biggest difference between men and women?...what they mean when they say "I got through a whole box of tissues watching that movie..."

A wife said to her husband "The trouble with men is they can't multitask..." The husband annoyedly replied "Oh yes they can!" "Ok" then said the wife..."Give me an example..." "Well..." said the husband "When I was shagging you last night, I was thinking of your sister..."

A homeless person walks into a restaurant and asks for a toothpick. The waiter gives him a toothpick and the homeless person walks back outside again. A few seconds later another homeless person walks in and asks for a toothpick as well. He gets his toothpick and walks out. This occurs a third time only the homeless person asks for a straw. The waiter, getting annoyed says "how come you're asking for a straw and your other mates are asking for a toothpick?" The homeless person says "Someone threw up outside. I need a straw because all the lumpy bits are gone!!!"

What's the difference between Abu Dhabi and Dubai?...People from Dubai don't like the Flintstones but people from Abu Dhabi do...

What did the banana say to the vibrator?...Dunno why you're shaking, she's gonna eat me!

An epileptics favourite chocolate bar is a Twix...because Twix fits!

Hickory dickory dock,

Three mice ran up the clock,

The clock struck one,

The other two got away with minor injuries…

My ex-fiancee was a Raspberry ripple after a near fatal car crash…always liked that phrase in Cockney rhyming slang…she was a cripple.

Limeys get their name from sucking on limes…where do Cockneys get their names?

A gayman called Gilberts partner died, Sandro. Gilbert wanted to feel him squeeze out of his ass one more time so he got his ashes made into a curry and ate it.

Why do Letterkenny dogs have flat faces?…From chasing after parked cars…thick as pig shit everybody from LK lol just kidding.

What is the smallest hotel in the world?…A womans pussy…you have to leave your bag on the outside.

Every little helps…as the mouse said when he pissed in the sea.

His ass is so fat you could stand on it and cut his hair.

When do you know you're in love?!…She slaps you on the ass and says you're in love!

There's more finger prints on her ass than there are in Scotland yard.

What is a hooker with no legs policy?…Cash & Carry.

Jesus walks up to the Inn with a bag of nails and a hammer. The Inn keeper opens the door and Jesus hands him the hammer and nails and says could you put me up for the night?

I couldn't walk on water but I could swim through land.

How many press ups can I do?...All of them.

I don't do press ups...I push the world down.

Once I died...then I was alright again.

I was a Hollywood action hero for a while. I had a stunt double but only for the crying parts.

My father was once asked while waiting on a gurney outside an operating theatre by a priest..."going down today?"...He replied "Yes, but not all the way!!!"

Superman was flying over a sunkissed beach when he spotted Wonder woman lying naked sunbathing. She looked delicious. He got an instant hardon. He thought fuck it...I always wanted to fuck that woman and swooped down and rammed it up. He looked at her and said "It's me Superman, did you get a shock?" She laughed and said "Not as big a one as the Invisible man!!!"

Ole King McCole was a merry ole soul,

And a merry ole soul was he,

He sat on the rock,

And washed his cock,

As his balls floated out to sea!

There was a young woman from Madrid,

Who swore she'd never be rid,

Until along came an Italian,

With balls like a Stallion,

And rode her like Billy the Kid!

Letterkenny women only wear knickers to keep their ankles warm!!!

Kermit the frogs middle finger smells of pork!!!

The Comedian Frank Skinner (Check out his autobiography if you would like to get into Stand up) said this joke in his book. He was on stage talking about a male rape case. The assailant raped and murdered the victim. Skinner said when they opened the victim for the autopsy, he looked like a Chicken Kiev…

What does a Derry ghost say?...Boo hi!!!

What does a Derry Santa Claus say?...Ho ho ho hi…

My favourite dish in a Chinese take away is Cream of sumyung guy…

I just love my take aways…my favourite is Breast of Chicken without the nipples.

Two Tacos had a fight. One Taco turns to the other and says "I'm Nacho friend anymore!"

Two beautiful women are walking down a country lane on a lovely summers day. They're local gals. They spot big Paddy with his semi naked muscular body glistening in the sun as he ploughs the field without even using a tractor. He's just pushing that plough along. They scream in unison. Their pussys dripping wet for him. "Paddy!!!" They scream..."Do you feel like a big cunt?!" Paddy hollers back "Fucking right I do, I've just ploughed the wrong field…"

Yo mama is so fat, she broke her leg and gravy poured out!

Yo mama is so fat, all the photographs of her are aerial photographs.

Yo mama is so fat, her waist line is the equator.

My wifes vagina is so big…when she sits around the house, she sits around the house!!!

I was all delighted yesterday with my weight loss. I weighed myself and discovered I'd lost 3 grams. It was only seconds later I realised I'd dropped my Cocaine.

What has 'W' at the beginning and a 'T' at the end?…Yes it does!

A young rope said to the old rope…"Are you an old bit of rope?" The old rope replies "No, I'm afraid not…"

My friend mcConelogue is so miserable that if he found a plaster, he would cut himself just to use it!!!

A Scottish man was sitting drinking his whiskey when a fly flew into it. He picked up the fly and tapped it with his other hand and said "Spit that out ya bastard!!!"

What's transparent and lies in the gutter?…A Paki with the shit kicked out of him…

Why do Paki's not play football?…Because every time they get a corner, they open a shop.

How do you stop a Pakistani drowning?…Take your foot off his head.

What do you do if you see a Pakistani drowning?…Throw in his family.

When men Golfers get older, they start losing their balls.

Why do women have legs?…Did you ever see the trail a snail makes!!!

You'll be picking up those teeth with broken fingers!!!

A taxi driver was limp so his wife said pick me up at the pussy…

Woman says to a man…"Party in my mouth…wanna come?"

A girl once asked me "What attracted you to me the most?" I always say the same thing…"Your mind…" It drives them crazy…they say "Really?" I say "Yeah. I wanted to fuck your brains out!!!"

That nutcase of a man is one synapse short of a thought.

My father said he was bulimic…he just forgot to throw up…he was a fat cunt…lol.

He also said he wears his inner child on the outside.

My mother said I never got out of my terrible two's.

She also said my modesty is the one thing I boast about least.

I never enter into a battle of wits with an unarmed man – Uncle Neil

Uncle Neil always does this…ask him to clear a space for a woman to sit and he'll wipe his face.

How does the moon cut his hair?…Eclipse it.

I have mood poisoning…must be something I hate!

Uncle Neil used to be called Biscuits in the gym because of the thickness of the weights he put on the bar.

I brought a woman home to meet my father and mother. I said "This is Amanda…" My father jumped up and said "It fucking better not be!!!"

My girlfriend of the time rang my house. I was only 17. My Dad answered the phone. Michael Brolly asked "Is that Con the father or Con the son?" He replied "No, it's Con the holy ghost!!!"

Do you smoke after sex?...Dunno, I never looked.

A man of prowess used to have 6 inches and 1 wrinkle, now he has 1 inch and 6 wrinkles.

I used to have loads of money in the bank and piles in my pocket…now, I have no money in the bank and piles in my arse!

What do you give the man who has everything as a present?...Penicillan – Johnny Quigley

There's none more pure than a repentant whore!!!

I felt like a spare prick at a whores wedding.

What do you call the useless bit of skin around a womans pussy?...A woman.

Whats the difference between a snowman and a snow woman?...Snow balls.

How do you know the Coalman's been at your wife?...Her pussy is all slack.

Why is the space between a womans tits and her pussy called a waist?... Because there is room for at least another pair of tits there.

Woman should have 3 boobs. 1 at the back for dancing.

Binmen are always tossing their rubbish into other peoples bins because they do not like being binmen.

Golfers lose their balls when it rains because they do not like the wet grass between their toes.

Mud spelled backwards is Dum.

A woman said to her husband "I'm leaving you because of your OCD!" "Fine…" said the man…"Close the door 7 times on your way out!!!"

What's the last thing to go through a flies mind when it hits the windscreen?...It's asshole.

A wife said to her husband she wanted a boob job to increase her boob size. The husband said "Rub toilet roll up and down between them…" "Why?" said the wife. "What will that do?" "It'll make them bigger… just look at the size of your arse!!!"

When talking about getting a woman into bed say "Candy's dandy but liquor's quicker!!!"

A hooker was staying in a bedsit. The owner was always asking for his cut of her money. The next day after a new tenant moved in. There was a knock at the door. The new tenant was there, he had a monkey. The tenant was really horny and asked the hooker could he have a shag? The hooker said no problem. The lights suddenly went out and they went to the bed. There was a power cut. They went at it ferociously. The next thing the man said when are we going to start? The woman said I'm started already… (Uncle Charlie O'Donnell told me something similar when I was very young. I didn't get the joke and he had to explain it to me lol)

www.ingramcontent.com/pod-product-compliance
Lightning Source LLC
Chambersburg PA
CBHW030425120726
47903CB00003B/816